STORAGE

ACPL ITEM
DISCARD

3 1833 00512 6682

P9-EDO-443

Y FICTION

THE FABER BOOK OF ANIMAL
STORIES

DO NOT REMOVE
CARDS FROM POCKET

ALLEN COUNTY PUBLIC LIBRARY

FORT WAYNE, INDIANA 46802

You may return this book to any agency, branch,
or bookmobile of the Allen County Public Library.

DEMCO

THE FABER BOOK OF ANIMAL STORIES

THE FABER BOOK OF
ANIMAL STORIES

Edited with a Foreword

by

JOHNNY MORRIS

faber and faber
LONDON · BOSTON

First published in 1978
by Faber and Faber Limited
3 Queen Square London WC1
First published in this edition in 1984
Photoset in VIP Bembo by
Western Printing Services Ltd, Bristol
Printed and bound in Great Britain by
Whitstable Litho Ltd, Whitstable, Kent

All rights reserved

©This collection Faber and Faber 1978
©Foreword Johnny Morris 1978

This book is sold subject to the condition that it shall not, by way of trade
or otherwise, be lent, resold, hired out or otherwise circulated without the
publisher's prior consent in any form of binding or cover other than that
in which it is published and without a similar condition including
this condition being imposed on the subsequent purchaser.

British Library Cataloguing in Publication Data

The Faber book of animal stories.
1. Short stories, English   2. Animals—Fiction
I. Morris, Johnny
823'.01'0836 [FS]   PR1309.A/

ISBN 0-571-13281-2

Allen County Public Library.
Ft. Wayne, Indiana

Contents

2259316

Contents

Acknowledgements

Acknowledgements and thanks are due for kind permission to reprint:
Methuen & Company Ltd. for "Hank and Jeff" from *Mainly about Wolves* by Ernest Thompson Seton; David Stephen and the Lutterworth Press for "The Foumart of Ravenscraig Wood" from *The Red Stranger* by David Stephen; Joyce Stranger and J. M. Dent & Sons Ltd. for "Fire in the Forest" from *The Secret Herds* by Joyce Stranger; Hodder and Stoughton Ltd. for "Coaly-Bay, the Outlaw Horse" from *Wild Animal Ways* by Ernest Thompson Seton; Gerald Durrell and Collins, Publishers for an extract from *Two in the Bush* by Gerald Durrell; the Executors of the Estate of Mrs Elsie Bambridge and The Macmillan Company of London and Basingstoke for "Moti Guj, Mutineer" from *Life's Handicap* by Rudyard Kipling; Major George Bruce and William Blackwood & Sons Ltd. for "Natuk" which first appeared in *Blackwood's Magazine*; Blackie & Son Ltd. for "The Loons of Thunder Bay" from *Wild and Free* by H. Mortimer Batten; Frank Penn-Smith and Chatto & Windus for "Destiny" from *Hang!* by Frank Penn-Smith; Henry Williamson and Macdonald & Jane's for "The Heller" from *Collected Nature Stories* by Henry Williamson; David Attenborough and the Lutterworth Press for an extract from the abridged edition of *Zoo Quest for a Dragon* by David Attenborough; Eyre & Spottiswoode Ltd. for "Home Life of a Holy Cat" from *Laura was my Camel* by

Arthur Weigall; James Herriot and Michael Joseph Ltd. for an excerpt from *It Shouldn't Happen to a Vet* by James Herriot; the Society of Authors as the literary representative of the Estate of John Masefield for "The Seal Man" and "Port of Many Ships" from *A Mainsail Haul* by John Masefield published by Rupert Hart-Davis. For an extract from *Never Cry Wolf* by Farley Mowat reprinted by permission of The Canadian Publishers, McClelland and Stewart Limited, Toronto, and Hughes Massie Ltd.; for "Under the Ice-roof" from *Haunters of the Silences* by Charles G. D. Roberts reprinted by permission of The Canadian Publishers, McClelland and Stewart Limited, Toronto. "Tookhees" is taken from *Beasts of the Field* by William J. Long; "Laura" is by Saki; "Concerning Cats" is taken from *A Shepherd's Life* by W. H. Hudson.

Foreword

Sometimes animal stories can be very boring indeed. We have all had to listen to them at some time or another. There is the dear lady who carefully relates in detail how her dear little dog spends every individual minute of its yappy day, starting early in the morning when the news-paper plops through the letter-box. How the sweet thing scuttles downstairs and brings the paper up to his Mum and yaps and yaps until she takes the lid off a little red tin that she keeps by her bedside and gives him his early morning choc-choc. Oh! he knows that little red tin has got choc-chocs in it. And then he has his saucer of milk with just a dash of tea. He won't drink the milk cold, oh no, he must have that dash of warm tea to take the chill off the milk. And then he asks to be let out. And he never goes out of the garden; even if the newspaper man has left the gate open he won't set foot outside without his Mum. And he's a wonderful little house-dog. He seems to sense that someone is coming a half a mile away, long before they have reached the garden gate. And his "warning" bark is different from his "asking" bark. Oh! yes, you know at once when someone is coming.

And the funny thing is he will let people into the house but let them try to get out! The number of people he has trapped in the sitting-room when Mum has gone to answer the telephone in the hall. They daren't move! Even when they so much as cross their legs he snarls and curls his lip to show that deadly dangerous fang. But not

11

with children. Children can do anything with him. Dress him up, carry him around the garden, put him in a doll's pram. Need I go on?

Of course his Mum loves him. And he loves his Mum. His life revolves around his Mum; he regards her as his pack leader. The dog is descended from the wolf and still retains some of the wolf's characteristics. A pack of wolves has a pack leader. He is the boss, and he controls the pack. The others respect him, do as they're told and greet him when he moves amongst them. They do this by licking his face. We think a dog is being very friendly when he tries to lick our faces. He is indeed. He is saying "You're going to be nice to me, aren't you, because I know perfectly well that you are in charge around here and believe me I don't want any trouble." Of course, our faces are quite out of reach of most dogs and so they sometimes jump up to try to lick them. We don't like that because it dirties our clothes, and so the dog has to be trained not to jump up. This is not very difficult because the dog is very anxious to please his pack leader.

Some dogs regard practically all human beings as pack leaders, but others will tolerate only one leader. These, as you have heard, are "one man" dogs. And it is of these "one man" dogs that many stories are told. Now it all depends on how you tell a story whether you will hold your listener's or reader's attention. The lady with the little dog and the choc-chocs soon has her listeners yawning because nothing ever happens. And something should happen in stories. It is only when she says, "You know, he understands every word that I say" that someone might wake up and ask "Does he understand the words 'phenomenal' and 'juxtaposition'?" Well, of course he does not. Dogs do understand a few words of command and they soon get to know words like "Walkies". But what they seem to understand very well is the mood of the pack leader, whether he is angry, happy or sad. And this is perhaps what we appreciate most about the dog.

He understands our emotions and is sympathetic to them. Indeed, it would seem that since he has lived so near to us he has taken on these emotions himself. He too can be aggressive, cowardly, happy and miserable—in fact, all the things that we are. And we are a pretty tricky lot. The dog has changed quite a bit from his fine ancestor the wolf. The wolf is a shy animal and not a bit as he is depicted in so many fairy stories. He is not the treacherous villain that he's made out to be. It is true that he is a hunter and that he kills, but his behaviour is fairly predictable and as far as is known there is no record of a pack of wolves attacking human beings.

The same cannot be said of the humanised wolf—the dog. And this applies to all "tame" wild animals; they are much more of a danger to us than wild animals. A tame wild animal has lost its fear of man and since it has lost its fear it will assert itself just whenever it feels like it. When a tame gorilla asserts itself it can hurt quite a lot. Even a tiny tame animal can create a little havoc when it asserts itself.

We once used a ring-tailed lemur on the television programme "Animal Magic". She was a charming little animal, and I had known her for several years, in fact, ever since she was a baby. But you dare not argue with her. She lived, and still does, at Bristol Zoo and more than one keeper had to go on sick leave after one of her tantrums. Fifteen or more stitches were usually required to sew the unfortunate keeper up. I was more than careful not to let her find fault with me.

She appeared on the programme every week, and when she had babies, this time twins, they came along as well. I kept them happy with little sweets, grapes, bananas and, when in season, the foliage of young carrots. They liked that very much and they prospered and grew. In fact, the babies grew so big that you had a job to tell them apart from their mother.

Now, Mum always sat on my left shoulder when I closed the programme. It was quite easy to get her there because she knew that I kept the goodies in my left-hand pocket. The twins sat on my right shoulder because that's where Mum told them to sit and behave themselves. I always kept Mum very well supplied with sweets and grapes, partly to keep her happy and partly to prevent her from wandering off out of the picture. But one day I made a mistake. There is a very fine saying, "If it can happen, it will". It did. I got bitten.

As I say, it was almost impossible to tell Mum apart from the twins, they had grown so big. They had also grown in character, for on this particular day one of the twins decided that he had suffered long enough the dominance of his mother.

He chose to sit on my left shoulder. The other twin and Mother, ousted from her usual place, were on my right shoulder. This I did not know, for if you are looking straight ahead and talking into a camera you cannot tell exactly what is going on around your left and right ears. I kept feeding sweets and grapes to the lemur on my left shoulder, thinking it was Mum, and now and again making a little offering to the lemurs on my right shoulder. Mum was getting nowhere near her usual ration of sweets and grapes and she was becoming livid with me for ignoring her so callously. She exploded in a fury. I closed the programme with blood pouring down my face. Fortunately she did not give me the full treatment and I did not need stitching up. But I was very careful afterwards to make absolutely sure which lemur was which.

Different animals of course react in different ways should you not pay them sufficient attention. A dog will often put his paw on your knee and look at you with pleading eyes, begging for attention. Sometimes he will put his nose underneath your hand and lift it up to remind you that you haven't stroked him for at least ten minutes. But the cat is different.

The cat, whether it lives in the town or country, is a most adaptable creature. Should it feel any affection for the human beings it lives with, it will choose its own time to demonstrate that affection. One particular cat I had always ignored me when I came back after being away for a few weeks. He behaved as though I was still far, far away, walking past me in the garden without so much as a good morning (whereas it was his habit to rub along my leg if he met me). I used to think he might have forgotten me, but as he lived to be eighteen years old and still behaved the same way I am bound to believe he was deliberately showing that he did not approve of my leaving home like that. After a few days he would decide that I'd been punished enough and fetch up on my lap, purring a deep-down forgiving purr.

Dogs in general do not behave in this subtle way. The returning master, home from abroad, is often knocked flat on his back by a bounding Bonzo who is almost mad with joy that the Old Man has somehow brought off a miracle and returned from the grave. But the cat is different.

I once had a tom cat who led the life of a country gentleman. He came in regularly for meals and made it perfectly clear that he liked to sit at our table and listen to the conversation. You see, he appeared at our meal times as well as his own and his chair was always set for him close to the table. There he would sit with his black head and amber eyes just above the table, turning his head to whoever happened to be talking—and listening. There's no doubt that he knew all the family secrets and what we thought of one or two people in the neighbourhood.

Sometimes, however, there just wasn't enough room for him at the table, and although we always apologised that there wasn't a place for him he was obviously a bit put out. And when he was a bit put out he always went into the kitchen and sat in the kitchen sink. Why he chose the kitchen sink I'm not quite sure. But he was always there when we went out with the dirty dishes. It could be that he just wanted to show us what he'd been driven to, because there is no more uncomfortable place for a cat than the kitchen sink. He was a fine country gentleman. He did not brawl as tom cats generally do. He did not stay out all night. He was content with a comfortable home and good conversation. When we moved to another house he soon let us know what he thought about the place. He went back to the old empty home and sat and brooded. We used to collect him every day and take him to the new house, but he always went back to the old place. And on his way there one winter afternoon he was involved in a traffic accident and died. He was a cat that was attached to a place and did not want to leave it.

Not all cats behave like that. We moved home yet again with another cat, and in view of what had happened to our Country Gentleman we shut this one in a room in our new house. He simply screamed and swore at us. We let him out and he said, "Well, I should think so. Now please don't mess about, let's have a look at the place, shall we?" We showed him around, he inspected everything very carefully and then said, "Well, you've chosen quite a decent place, but you might have known that wherever you go I shall be more than delighted to go with you." And he curled up in front of the fire as though he'd lived there for ever. Some cats, it seems, are more attached to people than places.

He was attached to us because he had adopted us. He was a feral cat, that is, a domestic cat that has been abandoned or got lost, and has gone wild and lives on its wits. He simply decided one day that we were good enough for him, and moved in. I don't know how long he'd been living rough, but he certainly knew what was worth hunting and what was not. For instance, he would never touch a bird in the garden. Waste of time hunting little birds when there were young rabbits about. Our Mynah bird walked about in the vegetable garden, whistling and laughing, but the cat ignored him. Birds seemed to irritate him; they were fluttery frivolous things and if you've been a wild cat you just cannot be

16

bothered with frivolous nonsense, you've got to get on and keep body and soul together. He often used to look at me and then at the Mynah bird and blink. He just could not understand either of us. The Mynah bird for his part totally ignored the cat. He was happy enough in his own mystery world, strutting about the garden, picking up stones, putting them down again, laughing like a mad-man and talking to himself.

If you have ever met a Mynah bird you will know what very clear talkers they are. Their mimicry is incredible. One day a very serious gentleman came to the house and contemplated the Mynah bird for a long long time and listened to it talking. And then he said to me "Do these birds chatter away like this in the wild?" It's a nice thought isn't it? Imagine a wild Mynah bird waking up in the morning and saying to his neighbour "Hello there how are you then? Gosh, I had a shocking night last night, the missus has made a ghastly nest again, blinking twigs sticking in me back, didn't get a wink." The serious gentleman who imagined that Mynah birds spoke our language in the wild was very much out of touch with the animal world. We are a little more in touch with it nowadays, I hope. We are more aware of what we are doing to animals, of the species that have disappeared in recent years owing to our activities.

There was a time, not so very long ago, when we regarded all animals as our natural contenders for life on this planet. Forget what the Bible says about God's creatures, the hard facts are that some animals could kill you stone dead, some could poison and sting you, and pretty well all of them would either eat the crops you planted or trample them underfoot. There is no doubt that many people thought that animals were a great danger to us. All animals except the ones we domes-ticated and ate should be done away with. We placed animals at a very low level. And to a certain extent we still do. The animals that have things we want are made to give up those things without question. If they have fur or tusk or horn or hide that we want, then their end is in sight. Against us they have little chance.

At the other end of the scale we have the animal lover. I often get letters from people who write "Dear Mr. Morris, I am a big animal lover ... " Now what does that mean? A big animal lover. A very large person who likes and loves animals of all sizes or an ordinary-sized person who loves only whales, elephants and shire horses? Generally speaking, I find that the self-declared animal lover's range of affection extends to the cat, dog, budgerigar and New Forest pony. Nothing wrong with that, of course, for most of us have had dogs and cats that we've cuddled and loved and shed tears over. But nowadays we need a bit more than that if we are to be reasonable human animals and agree to share this planet with the wild animals. They are so close to us, they are so like us in many ways. For hundreds of years poets, painters and writers have used their talents to enchant us with pictures and stories of wild animals. The animal world is still a mystery to us. It is only natural that we should speculate upon their world, that we should invent our own interpretation of their behaviour. That we should be just a little anthropomorphic. This is a condition that is not appreciated by the scientific world.

Scientists say, "To call a lion a murderer is quite wrong. A lion is merely fulfilling its natural function in killing something for food." With this I would absolutely agree. But I have seen an *angry* lion. I think it only reasonable that we should be allowed to impose this human interpretation on a lion. I have seen many angry lions. I have seen suspicious tigers. I have seen frightened monkeys and playful dolphins and stubborn mules. Surely the strict measuring line of science must concede that in the animal world there exists a little of the human quality of emotion. For without emotion everything is dead. To which a scientist might answer, "What about bi-valves then?" Scientists can appear to be very boring to anthropomorphists.

Some of the stories in this collection were written many years ago. Many of them have a strong tendency to anthropomorphism. Some are factual, some rather fanciful, but all of them are written with a big broad view of the world and with intense observation and affection. As you will read, the world of the wood mouse, tiny though it may be, is just as fascinating as the world of the elephant, the world of the wild horse just as desperate, at times, as the world of the polecat. They have been viewed through human eyes and written down in human terms. They are regarded as our equals, as I believe they should be. But of course there is this extraordinary no-man's, no-animal's land that lies between us. What do they know about us? What do we know about them? They are frightened of us. We are envious of them. We wear their furs and feathers; we have learned to move on land far faster than a cheetah and to fly ten times faster than a falcon. But we still do not know exactly what goes on in the animal world. I hope we never shall. It is the mysteries of other worlds that engage our thoughts and do most wonderfully enchant us.

JOHNNY MORRIS

Tookhees The 'Fraid One

WILLIAM J. LONG

Little Tookhees the wood mouse,—the 'Fraid One, as Simmo calls him,—always makes two appearances when you squeak to bring him out. First, after much peeking, he runs out of his tunnel; sits up once on his hind legs; rubs his eyes with his paws; looks up for the owl, and behind him for the fox, and straight ahead at the tent where the man lives; then he dives back headlong into his tunnel with a rustle of leaves and a frightened whistle, as if Kupkawis the little owl had seen him. That is to re-assure himself. In a moment he comes back softly to see what kind of crumbs you have given him.

No wonder Tookhees is so timid, for there is no place in earth or air or water, outside his own little doorway under the mossy stone, where he is safe. Above him the owls watch by night and the hawks by day; around him not a prowler of the wilderness, from Mooween the bear down through a score of gradations, to Kagax the weasel, but will sniff under every old log in the hope of finding a wood mouse; and if he takes a swim, as he is fond of doing, not a big trout in the river but leaves his eddy to rush at the tiny ripple holding bravely across the current. So, with all these enemies waiting to catch him the moment he ventures out, Tookhees must needs make one or two false starts in order to find out where the coast is clear.

That is why he always dodges back after his first appearance; why he gives you two or three swift glimpses of himself, now here, now there, before coming out into the light. He knows his enemies are so hungry, so afraid he will get away or that somebody else will catch him, that they jump for him the moment he shows a whisker. So eager are they for his flesh, and so sure, after missing him, that the swoop of wings or the snap of red jaws has scared him into permanent hiding, that they pass on to other trails. And when a prowler, watching from behind a stump, sees Tookhees flash out of sight and hears his startled squeak, he thinks naturally that the keen little eyes have seen the tail, which he forgot to curl close enough, and so sneaks away as if ashamed of himself. Not even the fox, whose patience is without end, has learned the wisdom of waiting for Tookhees's second appearance. And that is the salvation of the little 'Fraid One.

From all these enemies Tookhees has one refuge, the little arched nest beyond the pretty doorway, under the mossy stone. Most of his enemies can dig, to be sure, but his tunnel winds about in such a way that they never can tell from the looks of his doorway where it leads to; and there are no snakes in the wilderness to follow and find out. Occasionally I have seen where Mooween has turned the stone over and clawed the earth beneath; but there is generally a tough root in the way, and Mooween concludes that he is taking too much trouble for so small a mouthful, and shuffles off to the log where the red ants live.

On his journeys through the woods Tookhees never forgets the dangerous possibilities. His progress is a series of jerks, and whisks, and jumps, and hidings. He leaves his doorway, after much watching, and shoots like a minnow across the moss to an upturned root. There he glides along the root for a couple of feet, drops to the ground and disappears. He is hiding there under a dead leaf. A moment of stillness and he jumps like Jack-in-a-box. Now he is sitting on the leaf that covered him, rubbing his whiskers again, looking back over his trail as if he heard footsteps behind him. Then another nervous dash, a squeak which proclaims at once his escape and arrival, and he vanishes under the old moss-grown log where his fellows live, a whole colony of them.

All these things, and many more, I discovered the first season that I began to study the wild things that lived within sight of my tent. I had been making long excursions after bear and beaver, following on wild-goose chases after old Whitehead the eagle and Kakagos the wild woods raven, only to find that within the warm circle of my camp-fire little wild folk were hiding, whose lives were more unknown and quite as interesting as the greater creatures I had been following.

One day, as I returned quietly to camp, I saw Simmo quite lost in watching something near my tent. He stood beside a great birch tree, one hand resting against the bark that he would claim next winter for his new canoe; the other hand still grasped his axe, which he had picked up a moment before, to quicken the *tempo* of the bean kettle's song. His dark face peered behind the tree with a kind of childlike intensity written all over it.

I stole nearer without his hearing me; but I could see nothing. The woods were all still. Killooleet was dozing by his nest; the chickadees had vanished, knowing that it was not meal-time; and Meeko the red squirrel had been made to jump from the fir top to the ground so often that now he kept sullenly to his own hemlock, nursing his sore feet and scolding like a fury whenever I approached. Still Simmo watched, as if a bear were approaching his bait, till I whispered, "*Quiee*, Simmo, what is it?"

"*Nodwar k'chee Toquis*, I see little 'Fraid One," he said, unconsciously dropping into his own dialect, which is the softest speech in the world, so soft that wild things are not disturbed when they hear it, thinking it only a louder sough of the pines or a softer tunkling of ripples on the rocks.—"O bah cosh, see! He wash-um face in yo lil cup." And when I tiptoed to his side, there was Tookhees sitting on the rim of my drinking cup, in which I had left a new leader to soak for the evening's fishing, scrubbing his face diligently. He would scoop up a double handful of water, rub it rapidly up over nose and eyes and then behind his ears,—on the spots that wake you up quickest when you are sleepy. Then another scoop of water, and another vigorous rub, ending behind his ears as before. Simmo was full of wonder; for an Indian notices few things in the woods beside those that pertain to his trapping and hunting; and to see a mouse wash his face was as incomprehensible to him as to see me read a book. But all wood mice are very cleanly; they have none of the strong odours of our house mice. Afterwards, while getting acquainted, I saw him wash many times in the plate of water that I kept filled near his den; but he never washed more than his face and the sensitive spot behind his ears. Sometimes, however, when I have seen him swimming in the lake or river, I have wondered whether he were going on a journey, or just bathing for the love of it, as he washed his face in my cup.

I left the cup where it was and spread a feast for the little guest, cracker crumbs and a bit of candle end. In the morning they were gone; the signs of several mice telling plainly who had been called in from the wilderness byways. That was the introduction of man to beast. Soon they came regularly. I had only to scatter crumbs and squeak like a mouse, when little streaks and flashes would appear on the moss or among the faded gold tapestries of old birch leaves, and the little wild things would come to my table, their eyes shining like jet, their tiny paws lifted to rub their whiskers or to shield themselves from the fear under which they lived continually.

They were not all alike; quite the contrary. One, the same that had washed in my cup, was grey and old, and wise from much dodging of enemies. His left ear was split, from a fight, or an owl's claw that just missed him as he dodged under a root. He was at once the shyest and boldest of the lot. For a day or two he came with marvellous stealth, making use of every dead leaf and root tangle to hide his approach, and shooting across the open

spaces so quickly that one knew not what had happened—just a dun streak which ended in nothing. And
the brown leaf gave no sign of what it sheltered. But once
assured of his ground, he came boldly. This great man-
creature, with his face close to the mouse-table, perfectly
still but for his eyes, with a hand that moved gently if it
moved at all, was not to be feared—that Tookhees felt
instinctively. And this strange fire with hungry odours,
and the white tent, and the comings and goings of men,
who were masters of the woods, kept fox and lynx and
owl far away—that he learned after a day or two. Only
the mink, who crept in at night to steal the man's fish,
was to be feared. So Tookhees presently gave up his
nocturnal habits and came boldly out into the sunlight.
Ordinarily the little creatures come out in the dusk, when
their quick movements are hidden among the shadows
that creep and quiver. But with fear gone, they are only
too glad to run about in the daylight, especially when
good things to eat are calling them.

Besides the veteran, there was a little mother mouse,
whose tiny grey jacket was still big enough to cover a
wonderful motherlove, as I afterwards found out. She
never ate at my table, but carried her fare away into
hiding, not to feed her little ones—they were too small as
yet—but thinking in some dumb way, behind the bright
little eyes, that they needed her, and that her life must be
spared with greater precaution for their sakes. She would
steal timidly to my table, always appearing from under a
grey shred of bark on a fallen birch, following the same
path, first to a mossy stone, then to a dark hole under a
root, then to a low brake, and along the underside of a
billet of wood to the mouse table. There she would stuff
both cheeks hurriedly, until they bulged as if she had
toothache, and steal away by the same path, disappearing
at last under a shred of grey bark.

For a long time it puzzled me to find her nest, which I
knew could not be far away. It was not in the birch log
where she disappeared—that was hollow the whole

length—nor was it anywhere beneath it. Some distance away was a large stone, half covered by the green moss which reached up from every side. The most careful search here had failed to discover any trace of Tookhees's doorway; so one day, when the wind blew half a gale and I was going out on the lake alone, I picked up this stone to put in the bow of my canoe. Then the secret was out, and there it was in a little dome of dried grass among some spruce roots, under the stone.

The mother was away foraging, but a faint sibilant squeaking told me that the little ones were at home and hungry, as usual. As I watched there was a swift movement in a tunnel among the roots, and Mother Mouse came rushing back. She paused a moment, lifting her forepaws against a root to sniff what danger threatened. Then she saw my face bending over the opening—*Et tu Brute!* and she darted into the nest. In a moment she was out again and disappeared into her tunnel, running swiftly, with her little ones hanging to her sides—all but one, a delicate pink creature that one could hide in a thimble. He had lost his grip and was left behind but he soon found the darkest corner of my hand and snuggled down there confidently.

It was ten minutes before the little mother came back, looking anxiously for the lost baby. When she found him safe in his own nest, with the man's face still watching, she was half reassured; but when she threw herself down and the little one began to drink, she grew fearful again and ran away into the tunnel, the little one clinging to her side, this time securely.

I put the stone back and gathered the moss carefully about it. In a few days Mother Mouse was again at my table. I stole away to the stone, put my ear close to it, and heard with immense satisfaction tiny squeaks, which told me that the house was again occupied. Then I watched to find the path by which Mother Mouse came to her own. When her cheeks were full, she disappeared under the shred of bark by her usual route. That led into the hollow centre of the birch log, which she followed to the end, where she paused a moment, eyes, ears, and nostrils busy; then she jumped to a tangle of roots and dead leaves, beneath which was a tunnel that led, deep down under the moss, straight to her nest beneath the stone.

Besides these older mice, there were five or six smaller ones, all shy save one, who from the first showed not the slightest fear but came straight to my hand, ate his crumbs, and went up my sleeve, where he proceeded to make himself a warm nest by nibbling wool from my flannel shirt.

In strong contrast to this little fellow was another, who knew too well what fear meant. He belonged to another tribe, that had not yet grown accustomed to man's ways. I learned too late how careful one must be in handling the little creatures that live continually in the land where fear reigns.

A little way behind my tent was a fallen log, mouldy and moss-grown, with twin-flowers shaking their bells along its length, under which lived a whole colony of wood mice. They ate the crumbs that I placed by the log; but they could never be tolled to my table, whether because they had no split-eared veteran to spy out the man's ways, or because my own colony drove them away, I could never find out. One day I saw Tookhees dive under the big log as I approached, and having nothing more important to do, I placed one big crumb near his entrance, stretched out in the moss, hid my hand in a dead brake near the tempting morsel, and squeaked the call. In a moment Tookhees's nose and eyes appeared in his doorway, his whiskers twinkling nervously as he smelled the candle grease. But he was suspicious of the big object, or perhaps he smelled the man and was afraid, for after much dodging in and out he disappeared altogether.

I was wondering how long his hunger would battle with his caution, when I saw the moss near my bait stir from beneath. A little waving of the moss blossoms, and

Tookhees's nose and eyes appeared out of the ground for an instant, sniffing in all directions. His little scheme was evident enough now; he was tunnelling for the morsel that he dared not take openly. I watched with breathless interest as a faint quiver, nearer my bait, showed where he was pushing his works. Then the moss stirred cautiously close beside his objective; a hole opened; the morsel tumbled in, and Tookhees was gone with his prize.

I placed more crumbs from my pocket in the same place, and presently three or four mice were nibbling them. One sat up close by the dead brake, holding a bit of bread in his forepaws, like a squirrel. The brake stirred suddenly; before he could jump my hand closed over him. Slipping the other hand beneath him, I held him up to my face to watch him between my fingers. He made no movement to escape, but trembled violently. His legs seemed too weak to support his weight; he lay down; his eyes closed. One convulsive twitch and he was dead —dead of fright in a hand which had not harmed him.

It was at this colony, whose members were all strangers to me, that I learned in a peculiar way of the visiting habits of wood mice, and at the same time another lesson that I shall not soon forget. For several days I had been trying every legitimate way in vain to catch a big trout, a monster of his kind, that lived in an eddy behind a rock, up at the inlet. Trout were scarce in that lake; and in summer the big fish are always lazy and hard to catch. I was trout hungry most of the time, for the fish that I caught were small, and few and far between. Several times, however, when casting from the shore at the inlet for small fish, I had seen swirls in a great eddy near the farther shore, which told me plainly of big fish beneath; and one day, when a huge trout rolled half his length out of water behind my fly, small fry lost all their interest and I promised myself the joy of feeling my rod bend and tingle beneath the rush of that big trout if it took all summer.

Flies were of no use. I offered him a bookful, every

28

variety of shape and colour, at dawn and dusk, without tempting him. I tried grubs, which bass like, and a frog's leg, which no pickerel can resist, and little frogs, such as big trout hunt among the lily pads in the twilight,—all without pleasing him. And then water-beetles, and a red squirrel's tail-tip, which makes the best hackle in the world, and kicking grasshoppers, and a silver spoon with a wicked "gang" of hooks, which I detest and which, I am thankful to remember, the trout detested also. They lay there in their big cool eddy, lazily taking what food the stream brought down to them, giving no heed to frauds of any kind.

Then I caught a red-fin in the stream above, hooked it securely, laid it on a big chip, coiled my line upon it, and set it floating down stream, the line uncoiling gently behind it as it went. When it reached the eddy I raised my rod tip; the line straightened; the red-fin plunged over-board, and a half-pound trout, thinking, no doubt, that the little fellow had been hiding under the chip, rose for him and took him in. That was the only one I caught. His struggle disturbed the pool, and the other trout gave no heed to more red-fins.

Then, one morning at daybreak, as I sat on a big rock pondering new baits and devices, a stir on an alder bush across the stream caught my eye. Tookhees the wood mouse was there, running over the bush, evidently for the black catkins which still clung to the tips. As I watched him he fell, or jumped from his branch into the quiet water below and, after circling about for a moment, headed bravely across the currents. I could just see his nose as he swam, a rippling wedge against the black water, with a widening letter V trailing out behind him. The current swept him downward; he touched the edge of the big eddy; there was a swirl, a mighty plunge beneath, and Tookhees was gone, leaving no trace but a swift circle of ripples that were swallowed up in the rings and dimples behind the rock.—I had found what bait the big trout wanted.

Hurrying back to camp, I loaded a cartridge lightly with a pinch of dust shot, spread some crumbs near the big log behind my tent, squeaked the call a few times, and sat down to wait. "These mice are strangers to me," I told Conscience, who was protesting a little, "and the woods are full of them, and I want that trout."

In a moment there was a rustle in the mossy doorway and Tookhees appeared. He darted across the open, seized a crumb in his mouth, sat up on his hind legs, took the crumb in his paws, and began to eat. I had raised the gun, thinking he would dodge back a few times before giving me a shot; his boldness surprised me, but I did not recognize him. Still my eye followed along the barrels and over the sight to where Tookhees sat eating his crumb. My finger was pressing the trigger—"O you big butcher," said Conscience, "think how little he is, and what a big roar your gun will make! Aren't you ashamed?"

"But I want the trout," I protested.

"Catch him then, without killing this little harmless thing," said Conscience sternly.

"But he is a stranger to me; I never—"

"He is eating your bread and salt," said Conscience. That settled it; but even as I looked at him over the gun sight, Tookhees finished his crumb, came to my foot, ran along my leg into my lap, and looked into my face expectantly. The grizzled coat and the split ear showed the welcome guest at my table for a week past. He was visiting the stranger colony, as wood mice are fond of doing, and persuading them by his example that they might trust me, as he did. More ashamed than if I had been caught potting quail, I threw away the hateful shell that had almost slain my friend, and went back to camp.

There I made a mouse of a bit of muskrat fur, with a piece of my leather shoestring sewed on for a tail. It served the purpose perfectly, for within the hour I was admiring the size and beauty of the big trout as he stretched his length on the rock beside me. But I lost the fraud at the next cast, leaving it, with a foot of my leader, in the mouth of a second trout that rolled up at it the instant it touched his eddy behind the rock.

After that the wood mice were safe, so far as I was concerned. Not a trout, though he were as big as a salmon, would ever taste them, unless they chose to go swimming of their own accord; and I kept their table better supplied than before. I saw much of their visiting back and forth, and have understood better what those tunnels mean that one finds in the spring when the last snows are melting. In a corner of the woods, where the drifts lay, you will often find a score of tunnels coming in from all directions to a central chamber. They speak of Tookhees's sociable nature, of his long visits with his fellows, undisturbed by swoop or snap, when the packed snow above has swept the summer fear away and made him safe from hawk and owl and fox and wildcat, and when no open water tempts him to go swimming, where Skooktum the big trout lies waiting mouse hungry, under his eddy.

The weeks passed all too quickly, as wilderness weeks do, and the sad task of breaking camp lay just before us. But one thing troubled me—the little Tookhees, who knew no fear, but tried to make a nest in the sleeve of my flannel shirt. His simple confidence touched me more than the curious ways of all the other mice. Every day he came and took his crumbs, not from the common table, but from my hand, evidently enjoying its warmth while he ate, and always getting the choicest morsels. But I knew that he would be the first one caught by the owl after I left; for it is fear only that saves the wild things.

Occasionally one finds animals of various kinds in which the instinct of fear is lacking—a frog, a young partridge, a moose calf—and wonders what golden age that knew no fear, or what glorious vision of Isaiah, in

31

which lion and lamb lie down together, is here set forth. I have even seen a young black duck, whose natural disposition is wild as the wilderness itself, that had profited nothing by his mother's alarms and her constant lessons in hiding, but came bobbing up to my canoe among the sedges of a wilderness lake, while his brethren crouched invisible in their coverts of bending rushes, and his mother flapped wildly off, splashing and quacking and trailing a wing, to draw me away from the little ones.

The little one that knows no fear is generally abandoned by his mother, or else is the first to fall in the battle with the strong before she gives him up as hopeless. Little Tookhees evidently belonged to this class; so, before leaving, I undertook the task of teaching him fear, which had evidently been too much for Nature or his own mother. I pinched him a few times, hooting like an owl as I did so,—a startling process, which sent the other mice diving like brown streaks to cover. Then I waved a branch over him, like a hawk's wing, at the same time flipping him end over end, shaking him up terribly. Then again, when he appeared with a new light dawning in his eyes, the light of fear, I would set a stick to wiggling, like a creeping fox, among the ferns, and switch him sharply with a hemlock tip. It was a hard lesson, but he learned it after a few days. And before I finished the teaching not a mouse would come to my table, no matter how persuasively I squeaked. They would dart about in the twilight, as of yore, but the first whisk of my stick sent them all back to cover on the instant.

That was their stern yet practical preparation for the robber horde that would soon be prowling over my camping ground. Then a stealthy movement among the ferns, or the sweep of a shadow among the twilight shadows would mean a very different thing from wriggling stick and waving hemlock tip. Snap and swoop, and teeth and claws,—jump for your life and find out afterwards. That is the rule for a wise wood mouse. So I said good-bye, and left them to take care of themselves in the wilderness.

The names used here for birds and beasts were given by the Milicete Indians—author's note

killooleet—white-throated sparrow

Hank and Jeff

ERNEST THOMPSON SETON

*A group of hunters about the camp-fire they were—and one
spoke about swapping dogs, much as he would horses or cows.
Then a silent man growled out: "No man ever gave up his
dog—if it was really truly his dog."*

*This struck a chord of memory in my heart and I told this tale
as it came to me long years before.*

It was in the wild romantic days of eighty years ago,
when the Ohio River flowed through unbroken, glorious woods, when Kentucky was one great game-field.
Here, on the lower Kentucky River, in his lonely cabin,
lived Jeff Garvin, a grizzled old hunter, with no company
but a big brindled bearhound whose name was Hank.

Very close were Jeff and Hank. Night and day their
lives were the same. They shared the same food and the
same perils. More than once when the hunter's arm had
failed, it was staunch old Hank that bore the brunt and
saved him. Never once had they been apart from the day
when first as a lubberly pup, Garvin carried him from the
mother's kennel.

Their living came from the woods and streams; deer,
bear, and wild turkeys abounded. When they wanted
meat, all Garvin needed to do was take down the trusty
rifle, call Hank, and within a mile or two their wants were
amply supplied.

In the winter, he trapped a few furs. These, with bear
and buckskins, were swapped at the trading-store,

twenty miles down the River, for powder, tobacco, tea, and such few things as the forest did not furnish for their needs.

In autumn, when the woods abounded in food, and the bears were fat, it was Garvin's custom to kill about twenty fine, black fellows, and smoke their hams for a food supply to carry him over next winter, spring and summer.

He was very expert at smoking hams. Garvin-cured hams were readily accepted by the trader on account. But a bear's ham is heavy, and four times heavy, when you must be your own packhorse over twenty miles of rugged trail through heavy woods. The hams, therefore, were used at home, "a speciality of the house", when rare strangers called, or a satisfying staple for himself and his dog.

It was in the fall of 1848. Garvin had stocked his smoke-house with twenty hams, mostly small, for these are best. The smoking had taken a month or more; but now that the nights were cool, the meat was safe. Garvin let the fire go out, and enjoyed the vista of smoky hams that greeted the eye as he opened the heavy door. Very heavy was that door of hickory splits, and strong as the walls that made the smoke-house, for there were thieves to be reckoned with—not two-legged—in those days, man was the scarcest animal in the country, except woman—but four-footed robbers—nothing less than the bears themselves.

There was no reason to fear them when Hank and Jeff were in the neighbourhood, but the hunter and his dog were often away for a week at a time. Therefore, the smoke-house was built like a pier-dock, with heavy close logs over, under and around. On the roof was a smoke-hole with a hatch that was hung nearly balanced with a pulley rope. It stayed where placed for a while, but slowly settled down unless propped. It was closed at other times to keep out small marauders; the walls and overhang kept bears away.

Hank and Jeff

It was early in November when Garvin went in to pick a ham for use. He was surprised to see that one of the pegs was empty. He counted the hams—there were but nineteen. He looked about carefully. There were no signs of burglary; doors, walls and roof were all in perfect order. He searched about for tracks, but found none.

He called Hank. The dog was busy chewing an old bear skull, and came slowly.

"Here, Hank, smell him out. Sic 'em. Where is he?"

The dog obeyed, sniffed all about the cabin, and circled farther off; then without apparent interest went back to the bear skull. Garvin was puzzled, and asked himself whether there were really twenty hams; maybe he had miscounted. But no—all honest bears wear their hams in pairs, and here was an odd ham.

Their cabin door was only loosely closed at night. Hank slept on a bear-skin by his master's couch. At the slightest noise, he would get up, scratch the door open, and challenge or assail any creature, man or beast, that might on rare occasions come near. It seemed impossible for a burglar to enter the smoke-house, which was close by. The mystery was unexplained.

Three days later, Garvin entered the place and found another ham gone. Again he sought for clues, again he and the dog searched all about for tracks. They found none, and soon Hank returned to an old bear-hide that he had been chewing behind the cabin.

A few days afterwards, Garvin and Hank set out towards the mountains on a preliminary trapping-round, making a few deadfalls ready, so they would be purged of the man-taint by rain, and weathered before the cold winter should come and make trapping profitable.

That night, as they were about to turn in by the campfire, they were aroused by the scream of a panther not far away. They were familiar with these unearthly yells and quite unafraid. But there was a strange new note in this; at times it was like the agonizing scream of a mad woman.

Hank rushed off, baying loud defiance to the challenge.

And soon the sound of the baying hound and the scream-
ing panther died away.

Hank was gone so long that Garvin fell asleep. In the
morning, the dog was back, apparently unharmed, but
seeming dull and listless. Jeff offered him some venison,
part of his own meal, but the dog seemed not hungry. He
barely mouthed the juicy steak.

There was something disquieting about the whole
affair. Garvin could not help remembering that an Indian
devil was said to haunt these hills; and some of those yells
were unlike any panther call he had ever heard.

Instead of going farther into the hills, he turned
homeward, and by afternoon was back at his cabin. A
general inspection showed another ham gone. Garvin
was furious now. He scouted about for tracks, without
success. He and Hank quartered the ground near and far,
but they found nothing unusual. The smoke-house door
was untouched, the house intact, and yet another ham
was gone. There were no bear tracks or man tracks near,
and Hank was much more interested in mauling that old
bear skull with gritting teeth and rolling eyes than in
searching for an impossible track.

That night, Garvin was deeply depressed. He cleaned
his rifle, and smoked long and idly. He had heard often of
spooks and warlocks in the Kentucky Mountains not so
far away. He had heard of Indian Devils, Catamounts and
Medicine Bears. And all of these weird creatures for once
seemed almost real in the light of recent doings. For they
seemed the only explanation of the continual losses and
that uncanny voice.

Hank, too, seemed deeply moved by something of the
sort. He curled his brawny brown form on the bear-skin
as usual, and slept. But his sleep was broken with short
whines and twitchings of his legs. Once or twice, he
yelped as though in pain. So Garvin muttered at last: "I
wonder if that cussed panther hurt him, or maybe he's
got spiked."

He examined the dog's body and limbs, but found no

injury. Hank responded to this care by licking his master's hand; then curled up again for slumber.

But his sleep was broken and fitful as before. Garvin
himself was wakeful. He sat up in his bunk, and something like superstitious fear possessed him as he watched
the indomitable old bearhound tremble and whine in his
sleep.

As Garvin stared uneasily, a thought came to him.
"That old Indian Medicine Man at Scioto put me up to a
dodge that will tell what a dog is dreaming—a way to
make you have the same dream."

He reached for his big red bandanna hanging on a pair
of deer horns, he softly spread it out on the head of the
sleeping hound, left it for five or ten minutes; then, lying
flat on his back, he spread the bandanna on his own face.

He fell asleep and dreamed that he was a dog, that
indeed he was Hank, the companion of the bear hunter.
He dreamed that he rose from his bear-skin in the night,
went softly to his master's bunk, poked his moist snout in
the face of the sleeping man, listened for a time, then
softly went to the cabin door. Deftly opening it, he made
for the smoke-house.

Six feet away was a tall pine-stump. He leaped on this,
then with a mighty spring landed on the roof of the
smoker. Near the top was the hung hatch. He thrust his
nose under the edge and raised it; then reached his long
powerful neck and plucked the nearest ham from its
peg, drew it through the smoke-hole, then down and
away.

The hatch closed of its own weight. He carried the
plunder off to a cedar swamp some forty rods away, and
there feasted to repletion on the meat he loved the most.
He could not eat it all; and what was left, he buried in the
black muck, digging a hole with his paws but rooting the
earth back with his nose till the meat was covered.

Garvin slept late. When he awoke, the dog was still on
the rug. The door was a little open, which might mean
that the dog had been out chasing some prowling beast.

For, though Hank could open the door, he never was known to shut it. And oftentimes, the door was left open all night, so that proved nothing.

His dream was strong upon him as Garvin went out. He opened the smoke-house to find *another ham gone*. His lips were tight, his jaw set, as he glanced towards the cabin, to note that Hank was again mauling the old bear skull as though that were to blame. Garvin went on alone to the cedar swamp. He saw Hank watching, even while pretending to maul the skull.

Every stump and tree was familiar through his dream, and he went direct to the cedar bush. There were signs of recent disturbance. He dug fiercely with his fingers. Soon he unearthed a bone—then another—bear bones—ham bones—then—part of the last ham!

He stood up straight. He gasped, "My God." He glanced furiously towards the cabin, and gave a familiar whistle. But no Hank came joyously bounding. He strode quickly back, to see the dog disappearing in the bushes.

"Come here, you," he yelled. The dog came cowering and whimpering. "Come right along."

He marched back to the swamp-hole, Hank slinking behind. There he turned to the dog, and pointing to the bone, said in a voice of thunder: "See that? So it was you all the time. You that was my pard. You that I trusted. Hank, you're a traitor. You're wuss'n a thief; you're a traitor."

The dog grovelled at his feet, whined, licked his boot. Jeff spurned him.

"You damned traitor!" Hank raised his big strong head just a little, and howled a very wail of death. He tried to reach his master's feet. The hunter kicked him off, muttering an oath.

"You traitor! Now you come and get what's coming to you!" He strode back to the cabin. Hank slunk far behind in an agony of shame and humiliation.

Garvin took down the ready-loaded rifle, and came

out. Hank was grovelling twenty yards away, whining his shame and sorrow.

"Come hyar," yelled the man. The great hound crawled slowly to his very feet, and gazed with blinking eyes on the face he had loved so long and deeply.

Jeff levelled the rifle at his partner's brain, right between the big brown eyes, those bright brave eyes that had ever greeted him in love, that had never yet feared facing death when his master was in peril. And a deep revulsion seized the hunter as he glared.

"No, I won't," he gasped. "I can't do it. You are my dawg. But I'm through with you."

He flung himself on his fur-rugged couch, and sobbed like a child.

Inch by inch, the old hound crawled in, slowly, belly to earth. Inch by inch his velvet ears trailed the dust, and his hung lips slobbered on the sill. A little, little moan, he made just one. Slowly he reached the old familiar bearskin. His master's hand hung down from the bunk.

The dog reached humbly forward, and ventured to lick the hand. At once it was withdrawn, and the hunter sat up. Growling harshly, "You traitor!" he gave the dog a fierce kick. With no sound but the involuntary gasp, the hound crawled out of the door, then raising his muzzle he howled the mournful death-song of a dog that knows he is lost.

Garvin lay in silence for an hour; then glancing at the sun-streak on the floor that was his clock, he rose, took his rifle, slipped a bundle of meat into his wallet, and stepped out. Hank was sprawling with his noble head humiliated in the dust. He raised his big brown eyes, and moaned. He did not raise his head or wag his tail.

"Come on here, you traitor," said Garvin savagely; and away he marched for two long hours with his humbled partner following far behind.

At last they reached the Ohio River, and the steamboat landing. The *General Jackson* was swinging in to get wood. He had counted on this. The negroes were hard at work, carrying in the cord sticks. On the upper deck were travellers, well-to-do planters and their families. A tall Southerner, leaning on the rail, marked the picturesque group of the skin-clad hunter and the superb dog. He said: "That's a fine dog you got, my friend."

"The best b'arhound in all Kentucky," was the answer.

"Will you sell him?" said the planter.

"No," said the hunter savagely.

"I've taken a fancy to him. I'd give a big price."

"Not for any price," was the answer.

"I'd surely love to have him."

The hunter glared across the river in silence for a time, then abruptly said:

"Would you be good to him?"

"Yes. I'm a sporting man. I love a good dog. What'll you take for him?"

"I won't sell him," growled Garvin with savage finality. "But—if you'll be good to him, I'll *give* him to you."

The planter was surprised, but the dog was tied and led up the gang-plank, the leash was placed in the planter's hand, and Garvin returned to the dock.

"My name is La Pine of New Orleans," said the planter, with an air of one whose name is a guarantee of honourable behaviour.

The steamer swung out. High on the upper deck was Hank near his new master. With his back against a snubbing-post stood Garvin gazing at the open water widening between him and his dog. The old hunter's face writhed in an inner struggle, his eyes were blurred with tears so he could not see much; but he could hear, and the long agonizing wail that came from the upper deck went through his very soul.

He waved his arm to sign "Come back". He shouted, "Let him go. That's my dawg." But the steamer sped away.

He turned and travelled now as he seldom had before through the down-stream woods. He knew that twenty miles away was another wooding-dock. The steamer had to make forty miles to reach this point. He spared himself not at all. He covered that rugged twenty miles in little over three hours.

As he came worn and breathless and feebly shouting down the hill, he was just in time to see the *General Jackson* swing away with all the wood she needed.

The river-boys thought him a madman when they heard him. But the familiar explanation "He missed the boat and got mad about it" was enough.

"Where do she dock next?" was his question when he was calm enough to ask.

"She don't dock till she makes Memphis now," was all he could find out.

He went back to the cabin, broken-hearted. He tried to think it would blow over in a month or so. He would get another dog. Then the notion of that was loathsome. "There ain't no other dawg," he told himself, and hid his real feeling in mere foul language.

He stuck it out alone for a week. One bright morning, he girded up his thin loins, and set his long hunter legs striding till he came to the trading-store. He had brought what furs he could lay hands on, and everything that promised a little ready money. But his plans were vague.

He sat silently smoking by the open fire till Culberson, the trader, was unoccupied, and sat down at the other side of the hearth.

"Say, Jack," said Garvin, "when do the *General Jackson* come back this way?"

"Heh," said Jack, "you ain't up to date. She won't come back never."

"What?"

"Ain't you heard? She struck a sawyer the night after she left here, just below Memphis, and was lost with all aboard. Not a soul saved but the darky cook."

Garvin stared stupidly. Then in a cold way, he said: "Wished I'd been aboard her."

His unspoken purpose had been to go to New Orleans

42

to seek out his dog, and now the blankness and futility of everything was stupefying.

He had no plans. He could not live his hunter life without his dog, "and there ain't no other dawg".

He hated the thought of his desolate shanty. He hung around the "Corner" which, with the trading-store, the saloon, and one or two houses, constituted the settlement. After a month, his cash was gone and his credit in danger.

He sat about, gloomily silent, or muttering to himself. The men began to avoid him. He was pointed at as having "something on his mind—likely killed some one".

It was in the second month of his loafing that Culberson said: "Jeff, why don't you take a job? They want a mail carrier to cover the forty miles between Carrolton and Frankfort."

Tramping the lonely woods with a mail sack was more to his taste than steady labour. Thus it was that Garvin made the weekly trip, and thus he came to hang around Carrolton docks, and at length to hear much about the sinking of the *General Jackson*.

"No, sah," said a voice in his hearing. "They wasn't all drowned. They was one man as had a big dog. That thar dog shur toted 'im ashore."

"What did you call him?"

"Pine or Lavine or something like that."

"And went on to New Orleans?" said Garvin, with interest that almost scared the negro.

"Ah don' know. Ah 'spose so."

He went as a deck hand, but in two weeks Garvin was in New Orleans. The name La Pine was slowly sufficient. He stood at last in a big house, to be kindly received by the tall planter.

"Where is my dawg?" was the blunt and passionate opening.

Then he heard a simple tale. The sinking of the *General*

Jackson was all too true. Every passenger but one was lost. La Pine's big dog had safely borne him down the midnight flood to a friendly shore.

Arrived in New Orleans, he was made much of by the children, and responded to their friendship. But many times they missed him, and found him again down by the docks, watching some steamer coming in, watching and sniffing at every man who came down the gang-plank; or howling as it sped away.

Two months went by. Hank was an established member of the family, loved by the children. Had he not rescued their father from death?

And less often now, he went to the dock-front to wail.

But one day, a hamper arrived from a friend in the hills. When opened, it disclosed six smoked bear hams.

Hank entered the room as they were being displayed. He sniffed intensely, gave a short yelp and dashed out and away. On the lawn, he stopped and howled a heart-rending howl, then ran. When last they saw him, he was running like mad toward the dock.

La Pine mounted horse, and followed. He was too late to see it, but many witnesses there were.

"That big houn' dawg jes lep in the water when he seen that there steamer. Them men in that boat tried to pull him out, but he bit at them. He jes was plumb bound he'd swim under that steamboat, an' the paddles struck him and dar he is."

Yes, there he was, crushed, still warm, with battered body and a broken skull.

Pointing to a spot under the cypress trees, La Pine continued: "That's where he lies. We all loved him."

The hunter stared his wild animal stare. Slowly his words rasped out:

"He—were—mah—dawg—I didn't—oughter—done —it. I had oughter forguv him—like he would me. He were mah dawg. He—were—mah—dawg."

He turned and was lost sight of.

There is a little white stone in a place of honour under the cypresses and moss of New Orleans. Six months later, there was an unnamed, now-forgotten, mound two thousand miles away on the track of the Forty-niners. But no one knows that their histories were closely bound together. They are the graves of Hank and Jeff.

Who Was Watching Whom?

FARLEY MOWAT

The lack of sustained interest which the big male wolf had displayed towards me was encouraging enough to tempt me to visit the den again the next morning; but this time, instead of the shotgun and the hatchet (I still retained the rifle, pistol and hunting knife) I carried a high-powered periscope telescope and a tripod on which to mount it.

It was a fine sunny morning with enough breeze to keep the mosquito vanguard down. When I reached the bay where the esker was, I chose a prominent knoll of rock some four hundred yards from the den, behind which I could set up my telescope so that its objective lenses peered over the crest, but left me in hiding. Using consummate fieldcraft, I approached the chosen observation point in such a manner that the wolves could not possibly have seen me and, since the wind was from them to me, I was assured that they would have had no suspicion of my arrival.

When all was in order, I focused the telescope; but to my chagrin I could see no wolves. The magnification of the instrument was such that I could almost distinguish the individual grains of sand in the esker; yet, though I searched every inch of it for a distance of a mile on each side of the den, I could find no indication that wolves were about, or had ever been about. By noon, I had a bad case of eyestrain and a worse one of cramps, and I had almost concluded that my hypothesis of the previous day

46

was grievously at fault and that the "den" was just a fortuitous hole in the sand.

This was discouraging, for it had begun to dawn on me that all of the intricate study plans and schedules which I had drawn up were not going to be of much use without a great deal of co-operation on the part of the wolves. In country as open and as vast as this one was, the prospects of getting within visual range of a wolf except by the luckiest of accidents (and I had already had more than my ration of these) were negligible. I realized that if this was not a wolves' den which I had found, I had about as much chance of locating the actual den in this faceless wilderness as I had of finding a diamond mine.

Glumly I went back to my unproductive survey through the telescope. The esker remained deserted. The hot sand began sending up heat waves which increased my eye-strain. By 2:00 p.m. I had given up hope. There seemed no further point in concealment, so I got stiffly to my feet and prepared to relieve myself.

Now it is a remarkable fact that a man, even though he may be alone in a small boat in mid-ocean, or isolated in the midst of the trackless forest, finds that the very process of unbuttoning causes him to become peculiarly sensitive to the possibility that he may be under observation. At this critical juncture none but the most self-assured of men, no matter how certain he may be of his privacy, can refrain from casting a surreptitious glance around to reassure himself that he really is alone.

To say I was chagrined to discover I was *not* alone would be an understatement; for sitting directly behind me, and not twenty yards away, were the missing wolves.

They appeared to be quite relaxed and comfortable, as if they had been sitting there behind my back for hours. The big male seemed a trifle bored; but the female's gaze was fixed on me with what I took to be an expression of unabashed and even prurient curiosity.

The human psyche is truly an amazing thing. Under almost any other circumstances I would probably have been panic-stricken, and I think few would have blamed me for it. But these were not ordinary circumstances and my reaction was one of violent indignation. Outraged, I turned my back on the watching wolves and with fingers which were shaking with vexation, hurriedly did up my buttons. When decency, if not my dignity, had been restored, I rounded on those wolves with a virulence which surprised even me.

"Shoo!" I screamed at them. "What the hell do you think you're at, you ... you ... peeping Toms! Go away, for heaven's sake!"

The wolves were startled. They sprang to their feet, glanced at each other with a wild surmise, and then trotted off, passed down a draw, and disappeared in the direction of the esker. They did not once look back.

With their departure I experienced a reaction of another kind. The realization that they had been sitting almost within jumping distance of my unprotected back for God knows how long set up such a turmoil of the spirit that I had to give up all thought of carrying on where my discovery of the wolves had forced me to leave off. Suffering from both mental and physical strain, therefore, I hurriedly packed my gear and set out for the cabin.

My thoughts that evening were confused. True, my prayer had been answered, and the wolves had certainly co-operated by reappearing; but on the other hand I was becoming prey to a small but nagging doubt as to just *who* was watching *whom.* I felt that I, because of my specific superiority as a member of *Homo sapiens,* together with my intensive technical training, was entitled to pride of place. The sneaking suspicion that this pride had been denied and that, in point of fact, *I* was the one under observation, had an unsettling effect upon my ego.

Who Was Watching Whom?

In order to establish my ascendancy once and for all, I determined to visit the wolf esker itself the following morning and make a detailed examination of the presumed den. I decided to go by canoe, since the rivers were now clear and the rafting lake ice was being driven offshore by a stiff northerly breeze.

It was a fine, leisurely trip to Wolf House Bay, as I had now named it. The annual spring caribou migration north from the forested areas of Manitoba towards the distant tundra plains near Dubawnt Lake was under way, and from my canoe I could see countless skeins of caribou crisscrossing the muskegs and the rolling hills in all directions. No wolves were in evidence as I neared the esker, and I assumed they were away hunting a caribou for lunch.

I ran the canoe ashore and, fearfully laden with cameras, guns, binoculars and other gear, laboriously climbed the shifting sands of the esker to the shadowy place where the female wolf had disappeared. En route I found unmistakable proof that this esker was, if not the home, at least one of the favourite promenades of the wolves. It was liberally strewn with scats and covered with wolf tracks which in many places formed well-defined paths.

The den was located in a small wadi in the esker, and was so well concealed that I was on the point of walking past without seeing it, when a series of small squeaks attracted my attention. I stopped and turned to look, and there, not fifteen feet below me, were four small, grey beasties engaged in a free-for-all wrestling match.

At first I did not recognize them for what they were. The fat, fox faces with pinprick ears; the butterball bodies, as round as pumpkins; the short, bowed legs and the tiny upthrust sprigs of tails were so far from my conception of a wolf that my brain refused to make the logical connection.

Suddenly one of the pups caught my scent. He stopped in the midst of attempting to bite off a brother's tail and turned smoky blue eyes up towards me. What he saw evidently intrigued him. Lurching free of the scrimmage, he padded towards me with a rolling, wobbly gait; but a flea bit him unexpectedly before he had gone far, and he had to sit down to scratch it.

At this instant an adult wolf let loose a full-throated howl vibrant with alarm and warning, not more than fifty yards from me.

The idyllic scene exploded into frenzied action.

The pups became grey streaks which vanished into the gaping darkness of the den mouth. I spun around to face the adult wolf, lost my footing, and started to skid down the loose slope towards the den. In trying to regain my balance I thrust the muzzle of the rifle deep into the sand, where it stuck fast until the carrying-strap dragged it free as I slid rapidly away from it. I fumbled wildly at my revolver, but so cluttered was I with cameras and equipment straps that I did not succeed in getting the weapon clear as, accompanied by a growing avalanche of sand, I shot past the den mouth, over the lip of the main ridge and down the full length of the esker slope. Miraculously, I kept my feet; but only by dint of superhuman contortions during which I was alternately bent forward like a skier going over a jump, or leaning backward at such an acute angle I thought my backbone was going to snap.

It must have been quite a show. When I got myself straightened out and glanced back up the esker, it was to see *three* adult wolves ranged side by side like spectators in the Royal Box, all peering down at me with expressions of incredulous delight.

I lost my temper. This is something a scientist seldom does, but I lost mine. My dignity had been too heavily eroded during the past several days and my scientific detachment was no longer equal to the strain. With a snarl of exasperation I raised the rifle but, fortunately, the thing was so clogged with sand that when I pressed the trigger nothing happened.

The wolves did not appear alarmed until they saw me

begin to dance up and down in helpless fury, waving the useless rifle and hurling imprecations at their cocked ears; whereupon they exchanged quizzical looks and silently withdrew out of my sight.

I too withdrew, for I was in no fit mental state to carry on with my exacting scientific duties. To tell the truth, I was in no fit mental state to do anything except hurry home to Mike's and seek solace for my tattered nerves and frayed vanity in the bottom of a jar of wolf-juice.*

I had a long and salutary session with the stuff that night, and as my spiritual bruises became less painful under its healing influence, I reviewed the incidents of the past few days. Inescapably, the realization was being borne in upon my preconditioned mind that the centuries-old and universally accepted human concept of wolf character was a palpable lie. On three separate occasions in less than a week I had been completely at the mercy of these "savage killers"; but far from attempting to tear me limb from limb, they had displayed a restraint verging on contempt, even when I invaded their home and appeared to be posing a direct threat to the young pups.

This much was obvious, yet I was still strangely reluctant to let the myth go down the drain. Part of this reluctance was no doubt due to the thought that, by discarding the accepted concepts of wolf nature, I would be committing scientific treason; part of it to the knowledge that recognition of the truth would deprive my mission of its fine aura of danger and high adventure; and not the least part of that reluctance was probably due to my unwillingness to accept the fact that I had been made to look like a blithering idiot—not by my fellow man, but by mere brute beasts.

Nevertheless I persevered.

When I emerged from my session with the wolf-juice the following morning I was somewhat the worse for

---

*An alcoholic mixture to which the author had been introduced by an old trapper. Ed.

wear in a physical sense; but I was cleansed and purified spiritually. I had wrestled with my devils and I had won. I had made my decision that, from this hour onward, I would go open-minded into the lupine world and learn to see and know the wolves, not for what they were supposed to be, but for what they actually were.

During the next several weeks I put my decision into effect with the thoroughness for which I have always been noted. I went completely to the wolves. To begin with I set up a den of my own as near to the wolves as I could conveniently get without disturbing the even tenor of their lives too much. After all, I *was* a stranger, and an unwolflike one, so I did not feel I should go too far too fast.

Abandoning Mike's cabin (with considerable relief, since as the days warmed up so did the smell) I took a tiny tent and set it up on the shore of the bay immediately opposite to the den esker. I kept my camping gear to the barest minimum—a small primus stove, a stew pot, a teakettle, and a sleeping bag were the essentials. I took no weapons of any kind, although there were times when I regretted this omission, even if only fleetingly. The big telescope was set up in the mouth of the tent in such a way that I could observe the den by day or night without even getting out of my sleeping bag.

During the first few days of my sojourn with the wolves I stayed inside the tent except for brief and neces- sary visits to the out-of-doors which I always undertook when the wolves were not in sight. The point of this personal concealment was to allow the animals to get used to the tent and to accept it as only another bump on a very bumpy piece of terrain. Later, when the mosquito population reached full flowering, I stayed in the tent practically all of the time unless there was a strong wind blowing, for the most bloodthirsty beasts in the Arctic are not wolves, but the insatiable mosquitoes.

My precautions against disturbing the wolves were

superfluous. It had required a week for me to get their measure, but they must have taken mine at our first meeting; and, while there was nothing overtly disdainful in their evident assessment of me, they managed to ignore my presence, and indeed my very existence, with a thoroughness which was somehow disconcerting.

Quite by accident I had pitched my tent within ten yards of one of the major paths used by the wolves when they were going to, or coming from, their hunting grounds to the westward; and only a few hours after I had taken up residence one of the wolves came back from a trip and discovered me and my tent. He was at the end of a hard night's work and was clearly tired and anxious to go home to bed. He came over a small rise fifty yards from me with his head down, his eyes half-closed, and a preoccupied air about him. Far from being the preternaturally alert and suspicious beast of fiction, this wolf was so self-engrossed that he came straight on to within fifteen yards of me, and might have gone right past the tent without seeing it at all, had I not banged my elbow against the teakettle, making a resounding clank. The wolf's head came up and his eyes opened wide, but he did not stop or falter in his pace. One brief, sidelong glance was all he vouchsafed to me as he continued on his way.

It was true that I wanted to be inconspicuous, but I felt uncomfortable at being so totally ignored. Nevertheless, during the two weeks which followed, one or more wolves used the track past my tent almost every night—and never, except on one memorable occasion, did they evince the slightest interest in me.

By the time this happened I had learned a good deal about my wolfish neighbours, and one of the facts which had emerged was that they were not nomadic roamers, as is almost universally believed, but were settled beasts and the possessors of a large permanent estate with very definite boundaries.

The territory owned by my wolf family comprised

more than a hundred square miles, bounded on one side by a river but otherwise not delimited by geographical features. Nevertheless, there *were* boundaries, clearly indicated in wolfish fashion.

Anyone who has observed a dog doing his neighbourhood rounds and leaving his personal mark on each convenient post will have already guessed how the wolves marked out *their* property. Once a week, more or less, the clan made the rounds of the family lands and freshened up the boundary markers—a sort of lupine beating of the bounds. This careful attention to property rights was perhaps made necessary by the presence of two other wolf families whose lands abutted on ours, although I never discovered any evidence of bickering or disagreements between the owners of the various adjoining estates. I suspect, therefore, that it was more of a ritual activity.

In any event, once I had become aware of the strong feeling of property rights which existed amongst the wolves, I decided to use this knowledge to make them at least recognize my existence. One evening, after they had gone off for their regular nightly hunt, I staked out a property claim of my own, embracing perhaps three acres, with the tent at the middle, and *including a hundred-yard-long section of the wolves' path*.

Staking the land turned out to be rather more difficult than I had anticipated. In order to ensure that my claim would not be overlooked, I felt obliged to make a property mark on stones, clumps of moss, and patches of vegetation at intervals of not more than fifteen feet around the circumference of my claim. This took most of the night and required frequent returns to the tent to consume copious quantities of tea; but before dawn brought the hunters home the task was done, and I retired, somewhat exhausted, to observe results.

I had not long to wait. At 0814 hours, according to my wolf log, the leading male of the clan appeared over the ridge behind me, padding homeward with his usual air of preoccupation. As usual he did not deign to glance at the tent; but when he reached the point where my property line intersected the trail, he stopped as abruptly as if he had run into an invisible wall. He was only fifty yards from me and with my binoculars I could see his expression very clearly.

His attitude of fatigue vanished and was replaced by a look of bewilderment. Cautiously he extended his nose and sniffed at one of my marked bushes. He did not seem to know what to make of it or what to do about it. After a minute of complete indecision he backed away a few yards and sat down. And then, finally, he looked directly at the tent and at me. It was a long, thoughtful, considering sort of look.

Having achieved my object—that of forcing at least one of the wolves to take cognizance of my existence—I now began to wonder if, in my ignorance, I had transgressed some unknown wolf law of major importance and would have to pay for my temerity. I found myself regretting the absence of a weapon as the look I was getting became longer, yet more thoughtful, and still more intent.

I began to grow decidedly fidgety, for I dislike staring matches, and in this particular case I was up against a master, whose yellow glare seemed to become more baleful as I attempted to stare him down.

The situation was becoming intolerable. In an effort to break the impasse I loudly cleared my throat and turned my back on the wolf (for a tenth of a second) to indicate as clearly as possible that I found his continued scrutiny impolite, if not actually offensive.

He appeared to take the hint. Getting to his feet he had another sniff at my marker, and then he seemed to make up his mind. Briskly, and with an air of decision, he turned his attention away from me and began a systematic tour of the area I had staked out as my own. As he came to each boundary marker he sniffed it once or twice, then carefully placed *his* mark on the outside of each clump of grass or stone. As I watched I saw where I, in my ignorance, had erred. He made his mark with such economy that he was able to complete the entire circuit without having to reload once, or, to change the simile slightly, he did it all on one tank of fuel.

The task completed—and it had taken him no longer than fifteen minutes—he rejoined the path at the point where it left my property and trotted off towards his home—leaving me with a good deal to occupy my thoughts.

The Foumart of Ravenscraig Wood

DAVID STEPHEN

He came hurrying down through the barred and che-
quered moonlight of Ravenscraig Wood—sinuous, darting, rippling; leaping from mossed stump to black-
veined boulder; pattering along the brashed trunks of
fresh windfalls; a giant weasel with yellow cheeks, pale
lips and ears edged with white, masked and dark-furred,
with bottle brush tail. And, by all accounts, he had no
right to be there.

But he *was* there; he was no wraith. However, being a
polecat—called by some foul marten or foumart, to distinguish him from his relative the pine, or sweet, marten—there was a doubt about his pedigree, for the nearest
true polecats were supposed to be in Wales, several hundreds of miles away. Many people maintain that there are
no true polecats left in Scotland; others, more careful,
reserve judgement. This question of right polecats and
wrong polecats, which seems to me to be what it
amounts to, is worth looking at for a moment.

There may well be polecats left in Caithness; if there
are, they'll be full-blooded specimens. There *are* polecats
in other parts of Scotland, which may be the right kind or
the wrong kind. But there are polecats on Mull about
which there is no doubt at all: They are the descendants of
tame polecats, called polecat-ferrets, which became feral
many years ago on that island. These polecats are rejected
by the systematists because their lineage runs the wrong
way, as it were. But, for the life of me, I cannot see why a

57

polecat—because his ancestors once lived in hutches—is any less a polecat, than a Highland wildcat is a wildcat because one of his ancestors contracted a liaison with a domestic tabby.

The systematists used to claim that they could tell a real wild polecat from a feral descendant of the polecat-ferret by certain conformations of the bones of the skull. Now this is rejected. It is thought today that facial markings may be a true guide to identity. But it seems to me that a polecat that looks like a polecat, acts like a polecat, and breeds polecats which look like polecats, is a polecat for all practical purposes. The argument becomes academic if the polecat happens to raid your henhouse; real or *ersatz*, the result is the same.

The big dog polecat of Ravenscraig could have been real or an impostor, but I am not concerned about him here, for when he reached the drag-road through the timber he had to go sneaking up to the woodsman's hut and get himself caught in a gin trap—the same kind of trap which was responsible for killing off his ancestors over the greater part of Scotland. He hissed and chattered when the steel teeth gripped his paw, and his cries attracted the woodsman, who came out with a lantern in one hand and a faggot in the other and killed him with a sharp blow on the head. As I say, we are not concerned with him, though there was much argument about what kind of beast he was.

This story is about his mate.

Foumart, the bitch polecat of Ravenscraig, was smaller than her mate, which is the way of it with the true weasels. She was less than two pounds in weight, and barely twenty inches from her nose to the tip of her tail. In colour she was like him—dark purple-brown guard hairs overlaying pale buff underfur; but the patches between eyes and ears were less yellow and more grey, so that her masking was not so striking. Though less powerful, she was no less savage.

58

For some months she had been running with her mate, shifting ground regularly, and travelling by way of the glens; they had put range after range of mountains behind them. Now Foumart was plump, being heavy with young, and her wanderings were over for the present. She had already made her nest in a rock cleft, at 1,200 feet, in a birch thicket above Ravenscraig. It was a warm nest of dried grasses and rushes, which she had bitten off, or scraped together, and carried in her mouth.

The moon spotlighted her as she sat on the rock above her lair, in upright weasel pose, with bushy tail quivering; she was listening. Her breast was dark; she was more like a small wolverine than a big weasel. Her questing ears—supersensitive and highly selective—heard the hoof-swish of hinds among the trees; the light tread of a hare in the brushwood far up the hillside; the scurrying of voles in the deep of the heather; the claw-scrape of a cock capercaillie as he shuffled on his high pine roost in the wood. Foumart dropped to all fours and glided from the rock.

She crossed the hillside in a series of darts and scurries, sometimes bounding, but freezing every now and again to sit, with head up, listening. The moonlight did not betray her. She made use of every tussock, and heather clump, and pile of brushwood to conceal her movements, and when she sat bolt upright to listen she was just another dead, weathered piece of stick. The hillside was cleared forest, laned from glen to heights with layered branches—bleached, lichened, brittle. Foumart rippled over them, glided round them, insinuated her muscular weasel-body through them; she made no more noise than a vole might have made.

Her vision was poor, but her ears and nose were acutely sensitive, tuned to every nuance of sound or scent; she could have hunted blind. So she came on the curlew, brooding her four eggs in a wet, tussocky, hoof-marked lane between layered lines of brushwood. The bird was sleeping, with her long beak laid over her back. Foumart, hearing a movement as she burrowed her beak more comfortably into her feathers, twisted in her tracks and pattered towards the nest.

The curlew wakened when the polecat was almost on top of her. What she saw was a bristling fury, flashing white teeth. She knew fox and stoat, hedgehog and wildcat, but not this terrible grinning weasel. She leaped backwards even as Foumart's teeth snatched feathers from her neck, and lifted away with wild swish of wings, open-beaked and terrified, to throw about the sky in panic. Other curlews joined her, sweeping across the moonlit sky in shadowy flight, and their frantic cries could be heard by the woodsman in his hut beside the forest road.

Ignoring the bedlam she had set loose, Foumart spat feathers and pounced on an egg. She was smelling strongly of musk, its potency increased by her excitement: the musk-taint that is the mark of the weasels, and which is most powerful and overwhelming in the polecat. Cracking the first egg with her teeth, she bit through shell and membrane, shaking her head like a terrier with a rat, and ate the chick and its attached yolk-sac in a kind of frenzy. The second egg she opened more deliberately, spitting out the last fragment of brittle shell before she ate chick and yolk-sac without haste. Then, after sniffing at the two remaining eggs, she licked her forepaws methodically and washed her ferret-face like a cat.

Now she began to weave about, darting this way and that on her short legs, deceptively swift, supple as an eel: a weasel in every line of her, yet badger-like—seeking ... She knew what she was seeking, and she found it: a hole under an old, rotted root, corked by long weathering and parasites. After wriggling into the hole, and out again, she returned to the nest and rolled away one of the eggs under her chin, tossing it forward with her nose when it became lodged in a tussock. She pushed the egg into the hole, and went back for the second one. This, too, she rolled along and poked into the hole. She went in after it, squirmed about inside, then came out, shook herself, and glided away towards Ravenscraig Wood.

The vast wood was still in the revealing moonlight, damp and balsamy-fragrant, and, to human ears, silent. But to Foumart—gliding, bouncing, weaving round mossed stumps and running with muffled tread over the soft ground carpet—it was not silent; for above her own breathing and the whisper of her pads, which she could hear, there came to her ears the myriad sounds of the night: tread of rabbit and hare, mouse-squeak, the deep breath of a hind, the snort of a ewe, and the noise made by the ruffling of a woodpigeon's wings on a branch high overhead.

Through shadowy, light-chequered lanes of trees she leaped and ran—into old timber, unkempt, bearded with lichens, mossed and brooding—an eerie place, owl-haunted—where roebuck and fox trod their secret trails, where gaunt trunks of oak and corded ash, shorn and splintered to their waists by storm and lightning, crouched scarred and festooned: mouldering relics of a forgotten age. The polecat drifted through, wraith-like, flank to flank with her shadow, past the tremendous earthworks at a badger sett, and followed the well-marked trail of the brocks to the drag-road.

She ran the rutted drag-road, with its chips and saw-dust and scattered bark peelings, till she reached the tiered log-piles near the woodsman's hut. And up she had to go on to the first criss-crossed stack; up, then down again, then on to the next. She climbed well, but not expertly—not as expertly as a marten—and came down like a cat. She was on the stack by the woodsman's hut, weaving in circles, badger-like, sniffing, when it came to her on the air—musk-smell on a flaff of wind. It was the musk-smell of the dead dog polecat.

He was hanging by the neck from a pine branch that reached below the gable wall of the hut. Foumart couldn't see him, but she could smell him. Probably she knew what it meant. She snarled noiselessly, pattered back over the logs, and dropped to earth by the way she had come. She avoided the hut and, skirting the sawdust drifts on the slope to the glen, bounded down into the shadows.

Down there the Slainte rushed, broken and white-crested, over splintered ledges. The banks were rocky and steep, dripping water, and draped with woodrush. Foumart leaped and slid down the steep to the lip of the burn. With forepaws on a stone, and head weaving in circles, she looked across the rioting water, and knew the current was too strong for her. She would have crossed in an emergency, for she had no fear of water and was a strong swimmer; but there was no emergency. Back-tracking from the stone, she turned away upstream to the bridge and crossed by the parapet.

The moon was now slanting down the sky; soon it would be setting. Foumart raced from the glen, rippled across the forest road at the top, and was faced by the high deer fence, which was netted half-way to the top against rabbits and hares. She ran along the bottom of the fence, to left and right, padding at the netting with her fore-paws, then, realizing there was no way through, she climbed up it as if it was a ladder, gripping the meshes with her claws, and toppled over the holding strand into the planting of young Norway spruces.

The spruces were roe-high, crowded and interlacing, densely undergrown with thick grass, ling, bell heather and seedling birches; the undergrowth was riddled with vole creeps. To move silently in such cover was almost impossible, even for one as stealthy as Foumart, and the swish of her as she forced her way through the smother, parting the grass with her face, was heard by a moor owl on her nest in the heather twenty-five yards away. The owl hearkened, blinking her yellow and black eyes; she knew no vole was running there. But she was spared a death-grapple in the tall heather that night, for the sounds moved away from her and passed beyond her hearing.

Foumart cleared the young spruce planting and reached the edge of a roundel of mature trees where the ground cover was thin. There, in a few minutes, she pounced on two voles, killing them by a nip on the skull behind the ear. But she did not eat them. Instead, she snatched them up in her jaws and went leaping back down through the heavy cover of the planting, not troubling to conceal the line of her going. The moor owl on her nest long-necked in alarm, but again the sounds died away, and she settled back to brooding her well-filled eggs.

Haste was now driving the bitch polecat. She did not stop to sit up and listen. Down to the Slainte she slipped and leaped, and across the parapet of the bridge; then up past the wood-piles and into the deepening gloom of Ravenscraig. When she left the trees the moon had set, and when she crossed the open hillside, running the brushwood lanes, she was invisible. The curlews were still keening about their ruined nest, but she ignored them. The ground gloom was now deep enough to hide deer moving in line at twenty paces; beyond the pine-tops of Ravenscraig the sky was silvering. Foumart padded to her den in the rock cleft and squeezed in to her nest.

But not to stay! She dropped her voles in a side pocket of the rock-hole and came out again at once, breathing with lips parted and smelling of musk. Away through the birch scrub she scampered, swallowed in the ground gloom: the gloom that meant nothing to her because her nose and ears were better than her eyes. And curlews, grouse and peewits rose calling at intervals to betray her route.

This time she was not hunting aimlessly; she knew where she was going. Within fifteen minutes of leaving her den she was crossing the forest road again to the Slainte, but this time far out from the wood, in the open deer forest, where the wide flats by the burn were boggy and there were many small pools. There the soft peat was printed with the seals of otters, and deer came to scrape for a bite when the snow lay deep on the tops.

The polecat knew where she was going; she also knew what she was after. Out in the bog she padded, cat-footed, skirting the biggest pools, wading through the small and shallow. Her pattering feet plashed lightly in the puddles. All the time her ears and nose were alert for scent and movement.

Suddenly there was a *plop*! Then—snap! She had a frog. Snap-snap! She had another. They lay squirming, not dead. Foumart gathered them, gripping them by the thighs, then weaved from the bog with them dangling from her mouth. She had disabled them, without killing them: not like the queen wasp, who anaesthetizes caterpillars with her venom, but as the mole with earthworms, paralysing them with a bite.

Back at her den in the rock, she laid her frogs beside the dead bodies of the voles; and again she came out—this time to curl up on the entrance ledge and lick her fur. She licked and dozed till the sun cleared the sgurr behind Ravenscraig, gilding the great fang of Ben Dearg, turning the pines across the Slainte to pillars of flame and the pools on the flats to liquid fire. Out on the slope the blackcocks strutted, in brilliant crimson wattle, with ebony plumage glinting metallic purple, and when the Ben Dearg eagle came over low, banking steeply in the sun, his crown was touched with gold.

Foumart rose and crawled into the cleft. There was a dragging ache in her belly. Her time had come.

Five kits were born to the polecat in the nest in the cleft—five pale, ferret-like kits who made incessant demands on her breasts. Day after day she lay up with them, leaving them only for brief periods to void and drink, and in those first days she lived on the frogs and voles she had laid by before her kits were born.

On the fifth day, leaving them warmly curled up in the nest, she bounded down the brushwood lane to the root-hole where she had stored the curlew's eggs. The chicks in the eggs were chill and slightly tainted, but she ate them, leaving only the shells and yolk-sacs. This was the last of her stored food. Tomorrow she would have to hunt. But she had left the ground near her den little disturbed, so that she would not have to range far from her helpless kits.

During the next week she hunted Ravenscraig Wood, the cleared hillside and the glen of the Slainte, rarely ranging more than half a mile from the den in any direction. She killed rabbits, leverets, voles, a brood of young peewits, a slow-worm and a lizard. Her hunger was great and she fed heavily; but she was a wasteful hunter by human standards, killing more than she needed and sometimes not returning to a prey which she had only half eaten.

So man speaks of Foumart's kind as bloodthirsty, ravening Nimrods who strike terror into the heart of every living thing. Foumart was indeed a killer—savage, implacable, ruthless; she held nothing sacred. But what hunter does? What she could catch and hold she would attack; what she could kill she killed. She was merciless, as all the hunters of the wild are merciless, which means that sentiment was something unknown to her. And she killed more than she could eat, which is the cardinal sin, though not peculiar to polecats. But it would be wrong to accuse her of spreading terror far and wide on her range. Her victims knew fear when she was there in front of them—bristling, leaping, reaching for their throats: they did not spend their lives thinking about her.

Beyond all that she was a devoted and jealous mother, ready to fight to the death in defence of her kits, ready to challenge any trespasser even when they were not directly threatened. Put to the test, she would have faced man.

She came home one morning, when her kits were a fortnight old, with two voles in her belly and one in her jaws. She laid the vole in a corner of the den and came out to the ledge in front to lick her fur, and rest, for she was now liking spells away from her demanding family. It was when she was tongueing the fur of her breast that she saw the fox.

He came dawdling through the birch scrub, with no nonsense in his head and a hen grouse in his jaws: a big Highland dog fox, with brown legs and an enormous brush, travelling home with prey for his cubs. But his route was taking him below the rock where crouched the polecat, and the polecat immediately saw him as a threat to her kits. That meant she was ready to carry the war to the enemy.

Poor bewildered *sionnach*! The first he knew about the polecat was when she landed beside him, hissing and bristling. He whisked aside, drawing in his brush, but she came after him, *tissing* and chattering, reaching for his heels. That disconcerted him, for he was sensitive about his pads and his big tendon, so he ran twenty paces and stopped to ponder. But he was given no time to ponder, because she came bounding up to him again, flashing her needle teeth, and snapping at his feet.

Now he began to feel nettled. Though she was bigger than any weasel he had ever seen, he recognized her as one of the clan. He held weasels in contempt. Big though this one was, he was thirteen times her weight and could have broken her back with his long jaws. He had a feeling, however, that he was somehow trespassing, so he was prepared to be ordered away.

But, presently, he changed his mind. The more he retreated, the more she hustled him, running at him and snapping at him: a bristling, explosive stink-weasel with the hair of her tail on end. For three hundred yards he retreated before her without losing his temper; but his own den was now only a quarter of a mile away, uphill, and his anger increased as the distance grew less. Foumart was pushing close to the point where she would be the trespasser.

At the half-way stage the big reynard had had enough

of dancing and side-stepping like a big dog being harassed by a puppy. But he could not fight back with his mouth full, so he dropped his bird behind a boulder and turned to face her. And Foumart realized that the time had come to quit.

He was a master of the quick chop and flick of the paw, and he upended her once with a shrewd stroke. But, before he could get his long teeth near her, she somersaulted aside and clear. He followed her, poking at her and snapping at her back; he headed her and chopped at her mask, forcing her to turn; and once his teeth clashed so close that they pulled dark hairs from her rump. Foumart realized now that she was fighting for her life, and when she found a cavity under a rock she wasted no time scuttering into it. Even at that, his teeth almost closed like a trap on her bushed tail.

Now the reynard was satisfied; but Foumart was not. It was all against her fierce nature to miss an opportunity of striking back. Hardly had she drawn in her tail than, snake-like, she had turned about, and her masked face was at the entrance to the hole. The fox's muzzle was close, and she tried to bite him. Fortunately her teeth closed on air. If she had bitten him he would have tried to dig her out, or he might have waited for her coming out, and chopped her. But he was not bearing a grudge; neither his hide nor his pride was hurt; so he went away, picked up his grouse, and trotted to his den high above Ravenscraig.

Foumart peeped out when she heard him leaving; but it was some time before she came right out to go bounding down the brushwood lane to her kits.

The day was the twenty-eighth of May; the time six o'clock in the morning. The mists were sweeping, the sky grey with brooding clouds, the heather beaded with moisture. In the heart of a heather clump a little roe fawn was lying, with slim legs gathered under him and jet muzzle against his flank; he was twelve hours old, twice suckled. In the mist less than a hundred yards away his mother was standing over her second fawn. Of the buck there was no sign.

Foumart came pattering downhill from the heights with the wind on the side of her muzzle; up there she had killed a grouse and eaten half the breast. So she had no hunger for food. The roe fawn, however, was in her path—right on the line she was travelling. She could not see him; she could not hear him; and it is unlikely she could smell him. But she had to run right on to him . . .

The contact with the warm, breathing, quivering thing was enough for her. She flew at the fawn's throat, which was her way with prey too big to be killed by a single bite behind the ear. The prick of her needle teeth brought from him a wild cry, and he sprackled to his feet, staggering and trying to shake her from his neck. His struggles stung Foumart to savage fury, and she bit at him, and clawed at him with her feet. But his cries brought the doe.

She came up boldly, with forelegs flailing, but her first assault on the polecat was with her head. She butted Foumart from her hold on the fawn, sending her spinning into the heather, then followed up with fore-hooves dabbing. One blow from them would have smashed the polecat's spine, or stove in her ribs; but Foumart, realizing the kind of wrath she had called down on herself, kept rolling and twisting in the heather, and leaping away when she could. By a miracle she escaped the pounding hooves, and the doe, more concerned about her fawn than about vengeance, presently broke off the chase. When she pranced back to her fawn, who had by then fallen terrified in the heather, Foumart scampered downhill as fast as her short legs could take her.

But there was still the buck—savage, dauntless, and a perfect fighting machine—and when he saw Foumart leaping in the heather he bounded after her. Probably, although he had not seen the assault, he was able to associate the fleeing polecat with the plight of the fawn.

He attacked with the utmost savagery, pounding at Foumart as if he would stamp her right into the ground, and once he almost caught her off guard by prodding at her with his dirks. She felt the antler-tip graze her back, but she managed to wriggle away. Then, when she was dazed, panting and almost blind with rage and fear, she rolled into an old fox den—safe. The buck stamped round the hole for some time, and she could hear the hisses and hog-grunts of him, but, presently, the rage cooling in him, he too went away and she was left in peace.

Though uninjured, she was shaken. When she returned to her den she curled up with her kits and slept with them for some hours, nursing them as she slept. For the remainder of the day she lay away from them, near the den mouth, going in at intervals to nurse them, and it was long after midnight before she was pained by hunger and driven out to hunt.

The night was moonless, and the sky clear; the stars winked faintly. At that latitude there was no real darkness, and the polecat was a moving shadow on the hill. For an hour she hunted the ridge-top, catching only a vole, and then, when she was sitting up, in her listening pose, she heard sounds that were new to her. They came to her, now clear, now muted, with intervals of silence: cat-hisses and *ruckety-cooing* and a sound like the beating of wings. Foumart dropped to all fours and rippled down towards the sounds without further listening.

There were eleven blackcocks on the Lek. In full sunlight they would have been sable and ebony and iridescent purple, with bright crimson wattles; in the gloaming they were dark, indistinct shapes, visible only to the polecat in movement. Foumart bellied up to a pile of brushwood on the fringe of the Lek. The branches were grey and brown and silver, crusted with lichens; Foumart crouched among them and was invisible.

Some of the blackcocks were singing on their stances, with chests inflated; others were crowing, leaping as they crowed. The two birds nearest the crouching polecat were threatening each other, side-stepping face to face with lyre tails spread, then leaping at each other with hard slap of wings. They were unaware of Foumart's presence. She gathered her hindlegs when they began to side-step towards her, and when they were within striking distance she leaped to the attack.

She landed on the back of the nearer bird, clawing and biting, and he went down, hissing and flapping wildly, with her teeth in his neck. The second bird flapped up and away, in swift down-curved flight, towards Ravenscraig Wood. The other birds on the Lek, not knowing what was afoot, long-necked for a moment then returned to their jousting and crooning; perhaps they thought the blackcock across the Lek, beating his wings in death, was merely engaged in formal combat. Only when Foumart began dragging her prey to the shelter of the brushwood did they realize something was amiss; then they flew up, one after the other, and disappeared in the gloaming.

In the brushwood pile, Foumart tore glossy feathers from the breast of her still-twitching prey, and gorged herself on the dark flesh of the breast. When she was sated, her mask was crimsoned with blood. Afterwards, she had a mind to take her prey with her, so she grasped the body by the bared keel and padded away with it, holding her head high to prevent it from dragging. But the wings snagged in the layered branches, or trailed under feet, so in the end she hid the body under another pile of brushwood and went home without it. She had a notion that she would return to it.

That same day, at mid-morning, when larks were singing and cuckoos calling, the keeper saw the bloody feathers of the blackcock on the Lek, and wondered. Then his terrier found the half-eaten body in the brushwood, and he wondered still more.

Right away he thought of fox, which is what anyone would have thought of at first glance, but he was puzzled as to why any fox should eat half a blackcock in the open, then leave the rest, at the time of big cubs and big appetites. He rejected wildcat for the same reason; the cat would surely have carried the prey away. Then he thought of stoat, and decided it must be stoat, though still taken with the idea of an improvident or wasteful fox. Being a man who liked the quickest way of finding out about such things, he took a gin from his game-bag and set it beside the carcase of the blackcock. When he left, he was still wondering how the bird had died.

Foumart left her den while the sun was still red, and hunted the height in the purple shadows of the afterglow. She scuttered this way and that, sitting up every now and then to listen, without once hearing any sound to interest her; and when she turned downhill at last, remembering the blackcock, the last of the light—tenuous gold and apple-green and saffron—was gathered behind the mountains of the west. It would fade; it would creep along the line of the peaks; but it would not be extinguished.

She went down in great bounds, no longer hunting by stealth because she knew there was food where she was going. The crackling of rotten branches halted her suddenly while her prey was still a long way off, and she sat up, turning an ear to the sound, to place it. A mountain hare, lying downwind of her, closed his twitching nostrils on her taint and went crashing away in the gloom, but she kept her ear on the lesser sound which had greater meaning for her. Ignoring the panic flight of the hare she resumed her hurried scamper down the slope.

Her taint reached the brushwood pile before her, for she was running down the wind, and when she was twenty yards from the spot the crackling suddenly stopped. That meant she was expected. She approached stealthily now, and slowly, edging round the wind. Her ears could tell her nothing, so she was seeking answers with her nose. When she got the scent she bristled, for the scent was fox!

He was caught fast by a hindfoot in the keeper's gin, and had been crashing in the brushwood in his attempts to drag it away. In his plight he was in no mood to be chivvied by any polecat, so he showed her the colour of his teeth, which were stained with his blood. Whether Foumart knew it or not, he was the same big dog fox who had chopped at her after she had chased him from her den; trapped to a prey not his own on his first foray of the night.

The blackcock was still where she had left it, except that the keeper had wedged it down. Foumart glided in to retrieve it, prepared to defy the fox, but he chopped and snarled at her so savagely that her bold spirit was daunted. In his fury he bit at the restraining gin till he broke his tusks, then he lunged out at the circling polecat. Foumart knew then she was courting death if she tried to reach her bird, so she snarled at him, then glided away, leaving him to be knocked on the head by the keeper in the morning.

She was in Ravenscraig Wood, running in the damp ground gloom under the pines, when the light behind the mountains had spread half-way towards the point of sunrise. She had killed two beetles, which she had eaten, and a weasel, which she had hidden against necessity, and the hunger was gnawing at her.

Right down to the drag-road, then along the drag-road to the deer-fence gate, she hunted; then into the old timber of Ravenscraig, where she weaved about, darting and freezing in the muffled gloom. No rabbit or vole was moving, and she did not yet know of the warren on the far side of the timber. Back down to the drag-road she padded, sliding the last six feet sideways down the mouldy bank. In a wheel rut she paused to scratch an ear with a hindfoot. The light was becoming stronger minute by minute.

Foumart shook herself vigorously, crossed the road, and turned along the top of the steep slope to the Slainte, moving, with rump arched, in shuffles and scurries; and again you would have had the impression of a small badger running. She was homing, but still hunting, so she heard the sound clearly and reacted instantly. It came from ahead, and downhill—low-pitched, intimate, almost breathless: the *tooking*, vaguely owl-like, of a hen capercaillie.

Now the polecat moved with consummate stealth; silent and deadly. Forward and downhill she stalked, bellying low, creeping from mossed stump to silver fir and spruce, ever manoeuvring to keep obstacles before her to conceal her approach. Twice she dislodged pebbles which bounced with minute clatter downhill, but the caper merely blinked without turning her head. And, presently, Foumart was less than nine feet from her, slightly above and crouched behind the thick stem of a tall Norway spruce.

The hen capercaillie had three chicks wriggling under her and three struggling in splitting shells. The polecat couldn't yet see her, which is not surprising, for her plumage of black and white and buff and grey matched the withered leaves and dark twigs around her. But, feeling the chicks under her, she kept calling to them, so the polecat could place her by hearing. And, of course, she was very broody, which meant she had to recognize danger before she believed it, and be threatened before she moved.

Foumart gathered herself, padding for maximum thrust, and in two swift, unerring leaps was astride the capercaillie on the nest. The great bird—the biggest grouse in the world—exploded from her nest, scattering eggs and chicks down the slope. Huge and powerful, with a tremendous wing-stroke, she had no difficulty in launching into the air even with a polecat attached to the feathers on the side of her chest. She did not rise up; she went straight out from the face of the slope. And took the polecat with her.

That strange, terrible flight lasted perhaps two seconds, for Foumart had only a mouthful of feathers and, being airborne, could not bore in for a better bite. She was carried aloft, dangling, spinning, with the feathers twisting in her teeth. She could not have released her grip even if it had occurred to her. But the feathers ripped out with the strain, and when the capercaillie was over the Slainte, twenty-five feet above the rioting water, feathers and polecat parted company with her.

Kicking and spinning, Foumart fell: down, down, down, into the brawling Slainte, which at that point was deep. She hit the water with only a slight splash—a splash no greater than a leaping fish would have made— but the shock stunned her; so when she bobbed to the surface again, several yards downstream in the deep pool, her feeble, instinctive kicking could not prevent her from being carried away, choking and spinning on the smooth current.

Once clear of the pool, she was tossed and thrown and buffeted by the broken water, sucked under in the deep channels then emerging, coughing with the water in her lungs, to be rolled and battered in the rapids. She fought for her life, but the first stunning plunge had left her at the mercy of the water, and she was half drowned before her brain could direct her legs to swim. So she was carried down and down, under the deer fence and past the keeper's cottage, then through a narrow gorge, to be washed at last on to a pebbly sand-spit, and left there: battered, sodden and dead.

But that was not the end of her. Her body had to suffer the final indignity. The following afternoon the keeper found her, and carried her up to his vermin board, and with a two-inch nail he nailed her up by the neck beside the frayed, mummified and skeletal corpses of stoats and weasels, who were her kin.

Fire in the Forest

JOYCE STRANGER

The four boys had been walking all morning. It was time to eat. Malcolm was to gather the sticks, Davie was to fetch the water, Roger was to tend the fire and Paul would cook.

They looked about them. The serried mass of pines dropped away to the distant loch. It was very peaceful and very quiet. No one else existed.

The only sound was the wind that gathered in the trees, and sped round the heavy trunks, brushing the stiff branches. It had not rained for weeks and everywhere was dry.

So dry that Davie had to walk half a mile before he found a pool in the burn with enough water to fill the can. So dry that when Roger lit the fire the sparks flew on the air and caught the branch of a tree above him.

So dry that he could not beat the flames out. They spread and danced, and the little red specks of fire flew along the branches—and the boys ran. Ran to find the forest ranger and confess their crime. There were homes in the forest. There were beasts in the forest, and they had not known that fire could fly so fast.

The flames flew on the racing wind that was strengthening every minute. The wind had been biding its time, building up, running over the heather, speeding up the hill and chasing among the trees. It had been waiting to burst its strength in the sudden wildness of a summer gale, coming from nowhere, lashing the trees in the forest, lashing the wild waves on the sea loch, till the deep blue was patched with a smother of white, and foam fled across the rolling water.

The boys ran and the flames followed them.

The forester looked up, saw the fire, cursed and raced to the telephone. He called for the fire engines, and warned those who lived among the trees that there was danger. The houseowners were driving out of the forest even before the boys reached the fire post, and the distant siren sounded on the air.

They could not warn the beasts that hid among the tall trees.

Fire!

Terror tang and rank reek. The squirrel had known fire before, had seen his mother die in the flames. He fled down the hillside, caring for nothing but to escape before the blaze reached him, taking his family with him, his mate and the two young. Their urgent paws sped over the pine needles, running away from the wind and the fear, running towards the water, running towards the bare beach where the sea soaked the weed and nothing could burn.

Time was so short.

The wind was rioting in the bushes, flinging long streamers of blazing light ahead of it, thrusting merry fingers into every bush and tree. It sped the terror before it, blowing and gusting, so that yellow fire swept along dry branches, red sparks dived from bush to bush and danced on the air, a fountain of colour, alive and hotter than horror.

The stags on the mountain lifted their heads, and the pinpoint fire below reflected in their glowing eyes. They turned to run.

Crash through the heather, speeding hooves over the mosses, plunging through the peat hags, bounding over the rocks—a mass of frightened bodies thundering away from the blaze, in a panic-driven pack.

Halfway down the hill the hind herd joined them,

76

body pressing against body, eyes wild and ears flattened, white scuts warning as they bounded. The calves followed, close against their mothers, some so young it was hard to keep up.

On, speeding down the mountain. On, driven by the need for safety. On, not hearing the scream of the engines, not heeding the men who ran with brushwood brooms and axes, and felled the bushes in the hope that the fire would not leap the barrier. The men beat at the flames that darted towards them, seeking to smother the onrushing fires before they became too great.

High on the hill the wild cat heard the noise of burning; she knew the terror roar that raged in the trees and brought her kittens, running, racing, clambering over rocks, not down to the fire, but above it, climbing, climbing, while the little ones sped after her, striving to keep up with her. Every now and then she stopped and carried one, desperate to put distance between herself and the devouring monster that ravaged on the hillside.

She was the first to find safety, high on the peak, almost in the eagle's nest, under a ledge where water dripped and where the four kittens stopped to lap, and where she lay and guarded them lest they fall, or the eagle see them. She stretched and watched the hillside turn from green to gold and yellow and scarlet, to darkling smoke and bitter, choking reek. She could not find a clear space in which to breathe, and their eyes stung and the air was foul.

Then the wind took pity and turned away, and the air cleared around them. Smoke poured over the fire fighters, down towards the stampeding stags, among the squirrels and over the loch.

Fear. And the mountain hare was among the stags, racing among the hooves. He was kicked and beaten and bruised as he sought a way through, a way that would lead from the encroaching flames, and take him to safety. Bound and leap and bound again, with flopping ears and startled tail, with the tease and choke of smoke in his

77

throat, and the vision in front of him of the empty beach and the rolling water and the sanctuary away from the trees.

There were birds among the trees. Birds that flew with blazing feathers and plunged themselves in the tarns and streams where they could, knowing that water was their only hope. Birds that died as they fled. An owl that soared upwards, higher and higher above the forest, turned to the south away from the wind, and found his way to a distant moor. He cowered all night in a thorn tree and listened to the screams that sounded on the wind, and the roar, thunder, crackle and rage of the tearing fire.

Fire!

There were two otters in a holt on the hill. They stayed half the night in water, surfacing only to breathe, hidden and secret, and surrounded by smoke that almost choked them. But for them too came relief when the wind changed and they survived.

Fire!

Mice scurried into deep holes, but holes were not safe for burning leaves could fall and catch the grass, and many were suffocated. A mole burrowed deep and ever deeper, for the ground above him was hot.

The foxes went to earth with the badgers, deep underground in chambers dug long ago for other reasons. Fire could not come here, but some passages were sour with smoke, and the beasts within them had to find other beds on which to lie lest they choke and die. One vixen, young and not yet wise, took her cubs and ran with the stags. One cub was so severely kicked that he limped for months, and his mother and brothers had to bring him food.

Down the long hillside, with the fire chasing them, with flames leaping from tree to tree, from branch to branch, with the wind speeding and spreading and mocking man's small efforts. Down, away from the tremendous passion born from a tiny seed, from one small match, from a little heap of shavings, fanned by the shouting gale that hurled a tree from the ground, as its roots lay shallow. The tree crashed and within moments was a mass of glowing red, a heap of ash, a memory only. The wind flicked along its trunk and the small sparks drifted along the ground, and rose in columns as they reached yet another tree, yet another bush.

The eagles flew to another peak and rested, and watched the flames eat everything they had known. They watched the packed brown backs of the running stags and saw the darting hare, and spied the vixen, but fear held them captive and the beasts ran untroubled and no creature thought of food.

The little roebuck and his doe and twin kids flitted downwards, slipping among the tree trunks, the smoke driving them to distraction.

The herons left the heronry and flew south, and stood along the pebbled beach watching the trees, which they had known for centuries, crash to the ground and vanish in the holocaust.

Fire!

Smoke blackened the sky and darkness came early. The hillside crackled with the roar of flames, the crash of dying trees and the packed thunder of massing hooves. Down through the mossy rides, leaping the rocks, shouldering aside companions, eyes only on the clean wide beach and the raging sea that was now whipped by the wind to a frenzy so that waves shocked the shore as they broke and the foam scattered.

Noise was panic. Noise was terror. Noise was fear. Men shouted to one another as they worked, cutting the undergrowth, felling the trees, widening the fire rides, trying to contain the damage. In the fire station four boys sat and watched, appalled by the destruction they had caused in all innocence.

A gun sounded, and a flying bird dropped dead in a blaze of feathers. There were more guns on the hill. The boys dared not think of the animals trapped among the trees, of the smoke-filled burrows and the terrified wildlings. They had never imagined such horror.

"A dry summer and one small match!" the fire ranger said, coming into the room, taking a beef sandwich from a plate that one of the other men had made ready for him. He ate swiftly and drank, and was away again, without a word to the boys, who had looked silently at his blackened face and scorched hands, and found themselves without words.

Never light fires under trees.

If only they had listened, but now it was too late.

The tide was rolling in from the sea, and the beach was narrowing fast. Animals packed at the edge of the water retreated before the tide, except for two stags who swam with the waves and reached a small island where they crawled, exhausted and battered, and stayed for the rest of the summer and only swam to the mainland again when the need for the hinds took them.

The otters swam downstream and found themselves a new home, away from the forest. They did not play that night. Fear had exhausted them and, when they were sure they were safe, they curled together, pressed close for company, and slept. soon the female would be old enough for young. As yet she was too small.

When morning came the fire was only a grumble, a rumour in the sky, a trampled mass of blackened smoking earth, a deadening of trees from brittle branches that had lost their leaves, but not suffered more than scorching. The weary men continued to work, soaking the earth, beating down the sparks, watching till danger was past. No one had slept.

When the sun shone on devastation and the smoke was only a thin haze of cloud above the desolate forest, the fire ranger took the boys to the edge of the trees. They looked down on the packed beach where weary beasts lay side by side, red stag and hind and calf, roe deer and their kids, a fallow deer by itself in one corner, its antlers breaking the skin, the vixen with her cubs and the crouched hare.

The wind was gone. It whispered along the ground and brushed the blue silk of the waves and feathered them gently with foam. It stroked the fur of the crowded beasts, it seethed gently in the bushes.

The fire was dead.

The trees were dead.

The ground was dead.

The ranger drove the boys through the forest, saying nothing. There was no need for words. Davie had a burn on his hand and Roger had been struck by a burning branch across the face. None of them would ever forget.

"You can go," the ranger said, when they came to the edge of the town. He opened the door.

"Go?" the boys had expected punishment.

"You came to us and told us what you had done. And it was an accident," the man answered. "I don't think you need any other lesson."

They climbed out and stood on the path and watched the ranger drive away.

There was nothing to say to him or each other. They parted, each walking to his own home, each with a memory he wished he could forget but that he knew would stay with him as long as he lived. The memory of the running beasts, terrified by the horror that had been unleashed by one small match on the lonely hill where they had always lived their quiet lives, untroubled by man, browsing under the friendly shade of growing trees.

It would be a long time before trees grew again on the mountain.

Coaly-Bay, The Outlaw Horse

ERNEST THOMPSON SETON

Five years ago in the Bitterroot mountains of Idaho there was a beautiful little foal. His coat was bright bay; his legs, mane, and tail were glossy black—coal black and bright bay—so they named him Coaly-bay.

"Coaly-bay" sounds like "Koli-bey", which is an Arab title of nobility, and those who saw the handsome colt, and did not know how he came by the name thought he must be of Arab blood. No doubt he was, in a faraway sense; just as all our best horses have Arab blood, and once in a while it seems to come out strong and show in every part of the creature, in his frame, his power, and his wild, free roving spirit.

Coaly-bay loved to race like the wind, he gloried in his speed, his tireless legs, and when careering with the herd of colts they met a fence or ditch, it was as natural to Coaly-bay to overleap it, as it was for the others to sheer off.

So he grew up strong of limb, restless of spirit, and rebellious at any thought of restraint. Even the kindly curb of the hay-yard or the stable was unwelcome, and he soon showed that he would rather stand out all night in a driving storm than be locked in a comfortable stall where he had no vestige of the liberty he loved so well.

He became very clever at dodging the horse wrangler whose job it was to bring the horseherd to the corral. The very sight of that man set Coaly-bay agoing. He became what is known as a "Quit-the-bunch"—that is a horse of such independent mind that he will go his own way the moment he does not like the way of the herd.

So each month the colt became more set on living free, and more cunning in the means he took to win his way. Far down in his soul, too, there must have been a streak of cruelty, for he stuck at nothing and spared no one that seemed to stand between him and his one desire.

When he was three years of age, just in the perfection of his young strength and beauty, his real troubles began, for now his owner undertook to break him to ride. He was as tricky and vicious as he was handsome, and the first day's experience was a terrible battle between the horse-trainer and the beautiful colt.

But the man was skilful. He knew how to apply his power, and all the wild plunging, bucking, rearing, and rolling of the wild one had no desirable result. With all his strength the horse was hopelessly helpless in the hands of the skilful horseman, and Coaly-bay was so far mastered at length that a good rider could use him. But each time the saddle went on, he made a new fight. After a few months of this the colt seemed to realize that it was useless to resist, it simply won for him lashings and spurrings, so he pretended to reform. For a week he was ridden each day and not once did he buck, but on the last day he came home lame.

His owner turned him out to pasture. Three days later he seemed all right; he was caught and saddled. He did not buck, but within five minutes he went lame as before. Again he was turned out to pasture, and after a week, saddled, only to go lame again.

His owner did not know what to think, whether the horse really had a lame leg or was only shamming, but he took the first chance to get rid of him, and though Coaly-bay was easily worth fifty dollars, he sold him for twenty-five. The new owner felt he had a bargain, but after being ridden half a mile Coaly-bay went lame. The rider got off to examine the foot, whereupon Coaly-bay broke away and galloped back to his old pasture. Here he was caught, and the new owner, being neither gentle nor sweet, applied spur without mercy, so that the next twenty-five miles was covered in less than two hours and no sign of lameness appeared.

Now they were at the ranch of this new owner. Coaly-bay was led from the door of the house to the pasture, limping all the way, and then turned out. He limped over to the other horses. On one side of the pasture was the garden of a neighbour. This man was very proud of his fine vegetables and had put a six-foot fence around the place. Yet the very night after Coaly-bay arrived, certain of the horses got into the garden somehow and did a great deal of damage. But they leaped out before daylight and no one saw them.

The gardener was furious, but the ranchman stoutly maintained that it must have been some other horses, since his were behind a six-foot fence.

Next night it happened again. The ranchman went out very early and saw all his horses in the pasture, with Coaly-bay behind them. His lameness seemed worse now instead of better. In a few days, however, the horse was seen walking all right, so the ranchman's son caught him and tried to ride him. But this seemed too good a chance to lose; all his old wickedness returned to the horse; the boy was bucked off at once and hurt. The ranchman himself now leaped into the saddle; Coaly-bay bucked for ten minutes, but finding he could not throw the man, he tried to crush his leg against a post, but the rider guarded himself well. Coaly-bay reared and threw himself backward; the rider slipped off, the horse fell, jarring heavily, and before he could rise the man was in the saddle again. The horse now ran away, plunging and bucking; he stopped short, but the rider did not go over his head, so Coaly-bay turned, seized the man's foot in his teeth, and but for heavy blows on the nose would have torn him dreadfully. It was quite clear now that Coaly-bay was an "outlaw"—that is an incurably vicious horse.

The saddle was jerked off, and he was driven, limping, into the pasture.

The raids on the garden continued, and the two men began to quarrel over it. But to prove that his horses were not guilty the ranchman asked the gardener to sit up with him and watch. That night as the moon was brightly shining they saw, not all the horses, but Coaly-bay, walk straight up to the garden fence—no sign of a limp now—easily leap over it, and proceed to gobble the finest things he could find. After they had made sure of his identity, the men ran forward. Coaly-bay cleared the fence like a deer, lightly raced over the pasture to mix with the horseherd, and when the men came near him he had—oh, such an awful limp.

"That settles it," said the rancher. "He's a fraud, but he's a beauty, and good stuff, too."

"Yes, but it settles who took my garden truck," said the other.

"Wall, I suppose so," was the answer; "but luk a here, neighbour, you ain't lost more'n ten dollars in truck. That horse is easily worth—a hundred. Give me twenty-five dollars, take the horse, an' call it square."

"Not much I will," said the gardener. "I'm out twenty-five dollars' worth of truck; the horse ain't worth a cent more. I take him and call it even."

And so the thing was settled. The ranchman said nothing about Coaly-bay being vicious as well as cunning, but the gardener found out, the very first time he tried to ride him, that the horse was as bad as he was beautiful.

Next day a sign appeared on the gardener's gate:

FOR SALE
First-class horse, sound
and gentle. $ 10.00

Now at this time a band of hunters came riding by. There

85

were three mountaineers, two men from the city, and the writer of this story. The city men were going to hunt Bear. They had guns and everything needed for Bear-hunting, except bait. It is usual to buy some worthless horse or cow, drive it into the mountains where the Bear are, and kill it there. So seeing the sign up, the hunters called to the gardener: "Haven't you got a cheaper horse?"

The gardener replied: "Look at him there, ain't he a beauty? You won't find a cheaper horse if you travel a thousand miles."

"We are looking for an old Bear-bait, and five dollars is our limit," replied the hunter.

Horses were cheap and plentiful in that country; buyers were scarce. The gardener feared that Coaly-bay would escape. "Wall, if that's the best you can do, he's yourn."

The hunter handed him five dollars, then said:

"Now, stranger, bargain's settled. Will you tell me why you sell this fine horse for five dollars?"

"Mighty simple. He can't be rode. He's dead lame when he's going your way and sound as a dollar going his own; no fence in the country can hold him; he's a dangerous outlaw. He's wickeder nor old Nick."

"Well, he's an almighty handsome Bear-bait," and the hunters rode on.

Coaly-bay was driven with the packhorses, and limped dreadfully on the trail. Once or twice he tried to go back, but he was easily turned by the men behind him. His limp grew worse, and towards night it was painful to see him.

The leading guide remarked: "That thar limp ain't no fake. He's got some deep-seated trouble."

Day after day the hunters rode farther into the mountains, driving the horses along and hobbling them at night. Coaly-bay went with the rest, limping along, tossing his head and his long splendid mane at every step. One of the hunters tried to ride him and nearly lost his life, for the horse seemed possessed of a demon as soon as the man was on his back.

The road grew harder as it rose. A very bad bog had to be crossed one day. Several horses were mired in it, and as the men rushed to the rescue, Coaly-bay saw his chance of escape. He wheeled in a moment and turned himself from a limping, low-headed, sorry, bad-eyed creature into a high-spirited horse. Head and tail aloft now, shaking their black streamers in the wind, he gave a joyous neigh, and, without a trace of lameness, dashed for his home one hundred miles away, threading each narrow trail with perfect certainty, though he had seen them but once before, and in a few minutes he had steamed away from their sight.

The men were furious, but one of them, saying not a word, leaped on his horse—to do what? Follow that free ranging racer? Sheer folly. Oh, no!—he knew a better plan. He knew the country. Two miles around by the trail, half a mile by the rough cut-off that he took, was Panther Gap. The runaway must pass through that, and Coaly-bay raced down the trail to find the guide below awaiting him. Tossing his head with anger, he wheeled on up the trail again, and within a few yards recovered his monotonous limp and his evil expression. He was driven into camp, and there he vented his rage by kicking in the ribs of a harmless little packhorse.

This was Bear country, and the hunters resolved to end his dangerous pranks and make him useful for once. They dared not catch him, it was not really safe to go near him, but two of the guides drove him to a distant glade where Bears abounded. A thrill of pity came over me as I saw that beautiful untameable creature going away with his imitation limp.

"Ain't you coming along?" called the guide.

"No, I don't want to see him die," was the answer. Then as the tossing head was disappearing I called: "Say, fellows, I wish you would bring me that mane and tail when you come back!"

Fifteen minutes later a distant rifle crack was heard, and in my mind's eye I saw that proud head and those superb limbs, robbed of their sustaining indomitable spirit, falling flat and limp—to suffer the unsightly end of fleshly things. Poor Coaly-bay; he would not bear the yoke. Rebellious to the end, he had fought against the fate of all his kind. It seemed to me the spirit of an Eagle or a Wolf it was that dwelt behind those full bright eyes—that ordered all his wayward life.

I tried to put the tragic finish out of my mind, and had not long to battle with the thought; not even one short hour, for the men came back.

Down the long trail to the west they had driven him; there was no chance for him to turn aside. He must go on, and the men behind felt safe in that.

Farther away from his old home on the Bitterroot River he had gone each time he journeyed. And now he had passed the high divide and was keeping the narrow trail that leads to the valley of Bears and on to Salmon River, and still away to the open wild Columbian Plains, limping sadly as though he knew. His glossy hide flashed back the golden sunlight, still richer than it fell, and the men behind followed like hangmen in the death train of a nobleman condemned—down the narrow trail till it opened into a little beaver meadow, with rank rich grass, a lovely mountain stream and winding Bear paths up and down the waterside.

"Guess this'll do," said the older man. "Well, here goes for a sure death or a clean miss," said the other confidently, and, waiting till the limper was out in the middle of the meadow, he gave a short, sharp whistle. Instantly Coaly-bay was alert. He swung and faced his tormentors, his noble head erect, his nostrils flaring; a picture of horse beauty—yes, of horse perfection.

The rifle was levelled, the very brain its mark, just on the cross line of the eyes and ears, that meant sure, sudden, painless death.

The rifle cracked. The great horse wheeled and dashed

away. It was sudden death or miss—and the marksman *missed*.

Away went the wild horse at his famous best, not for his eastern home, but down the unknown western trail, away and away; the pine woods hid him from the view, and left behind was the rifleman vainly trying to force the empty cartridge from his gun.

Down that trail with an inborn certainty he went, and on through the pines, then leaped a great bog, and splashed an hour later through the limpid Clearwater and on, responsive to some unknown guide that subtly called him from the farther west. And so he went till the dwindling pines gave place to scrubby cedars and these in turn were mixed with sage, and onward still, till the faraway flat plains of Salmon River were about him, and ever on, tireless as it seemed, he went, and crossed the canyon of the mighty Snake, and up again to the high wild plains where the wire fence still is not, and on, beyond the Buffalo Hump, till moving specks on the far horizon caught his eager eyes, and coming on and near, they moved and rushed aside to wheel and face about. He lifted up his voice and called to them, the long shrill neigh of his kindred when they bugled to each other on the far Chaldean plain; and back their answer came. This way and that they wheeled and sped and caracoled, and Coaly-bay drew nearer, called and gave the countersigns his kindred know, till this they were assured—he was their kind, he was of the wild free blood that man had never tamed. And when the night came down on the purpling plain his place was in the herd as one who after many a long hard journey in the dark had found his home.

There you may see him yet, for still his strength endures, and his beauty is not less. The riders tell me they have seen him many times by Cedra. He is swift and strong among the swift ones, but it is that flowing mane and tail that mark him chiefly from afar.

There on the wild free plains of sage he lives: the

stormwind smites his glossy coat at night and the winter snows are driven hard on him at times; the Wolves are there to harry all the weak ones of the herd, and in the spring the mighty Grizzly, too, may come to claim his toll. There are no luscious pastures made by man, no grain-foods; nothing but the wild hard hay, the wind and the open plains, but here at last he found the thing he craved—the one worth all the rest. Long may he roam—this is my wish, and this—that I may see him once again in all the glory of his speed with his black mane on the wind, the spur galls gone from his flanks, and in his eye the blazing light that grew in his far-off forebears' eyes as they spurned Arabian plains to leave behind the racing wild beast and the fleet gazelle—yes, too, the driving sandstorm that overwhelmed the rest, but strove in vain on the dusty wake of the Desert's highest born.

The Three-Eyed Lizard

GERALD DURRELL

The launch chugged on for half an hour or so and then, through the spray-distorted windows of the wheelhouse, we could see two humps of rock on the horizon, rather resembling the large and small humps of a camel. I went out on deck and peered at our destination through the binoculars: the smaller of the two humps appeared to be nothing more than a desolate lump of rock, unrelieved by anything except the white frill of breakers it wore round its base; the larger of the two humps, however, appeared to have some vegetation on it, and at one end stood the tall shape of the lighthouse. These, then, were the Brothers, and it was here (depending on whether we could get ashore) that I hoped to see the reptile that rejoiced in the name of *Sphenodon punctatus,* or the Tuatara. Brian had sent a telegram to Alan Wright who, together with two companions, ran the lighthouse, asking him if they would (a) put us up for a couple of days, and (b) whether he could catch a couple of Tuataras for us. The reason for the last request was that now our time was growing short in New Zealand, and as we could only afford to spend a couple of days on the Brothers, we did not want to spend the time chasing elusive Tuataras to try and film them. In due course we had received a laconic reply saying that Alan Wright *could* put us up, would see what he could do about Tuataras, and would Brian please put ten bob each way on a horse called High Jinks, which was due to come romping home at about a hundred to

91

one in some race or other. Brian had been pleased with
the telegram but I had felt that the frivolous tone of the
whole missive boded ill for us. However, we were there
now and all we could do was to wait and see what
happened.

As we got nearer to the larger of the Brothers we could
see that it rose sheer out of the sea, the cliffs being some
two hundred feet high. On top of a flat area at the edge of
the cliff crouched what appeared to be a baby crane
looking, as cranes always do, like a surrealist giraffe. The
launch headed for the cliffs below the crane and we could
see a group of three people standing around its base; they
waved vaguely at us and we waved back.

"I suppose," I asked Brian, "that that crane's the way
they get supplies on to the island?"

"It's the way they get everything on to the island," said
Brian.

"Everything?" asked Jim. "What d'you mean by
everything?"

"Well, if you want to get on to the island you've got to
go by crane. There is a path up the cliffs, but you could
never land on the rocks in this sort of weather. No, they'll
lower the net down in a minute and have you up there in a
jiffy."

"D'you mean to say they're thinking of hauling us up
that cliff in a *net*?" asked Jim.

"Yes," said Brian.

Just at that moment the skipper of the launch cut the
engines down, and we drifted under the cliff, rising and
falling on the blue-green swell and watching the breakers
cream and suck at the jagged cliff some twenty-five feet
away. The nose of the crane appeared high above, and
from it dangled—at the end of an extremely fragile-
looking hawser—something closely resembling a gigantic pig net. The crane uttered a series of clankings, groans
and shrieks that were quite audible, even above the noise
of the wind and the sea, and the pig net started to descend.
Jim gave me a mute look of anguish and I must say

that I sympathised with him. I have no head for heights at all and I did not relish, any more than he did, being hauled up that cliff in a pig net slung on the end of a crane that, from the sound of it, was a very frail octogenarian who had been without the benefit of oil for a considerable number of years. Chris, wrapped up in his duffle coat and looking more like a disgruntled Duke of Wellington than ever, started Organizing with the same fanatical gleam in his eye that Brian always had in similar situations.

"Now I want you to go up first, Jim, and get the camera set up by the crane so that you can film Gerry and Jacquie as they land," he said.

"I'll go up next and get shots of the launch from the net, and then Gerry and Jacquie will follow with the rest of the equipment. Okay?"

"No," said Jim. "Why should *I* have to go first? Supposing the thing breaks just as I get to the top? Have you seen the rocks down here?"

"Well, if it breaks we'll know it's unsafe and go back to Picton," said Jacquie sweetly.

Jim gave her a withering look as he reluctantly climbed into the pig net, which had by now landed on the tiny deck of the launch. The skipper waved his hand, there was a most terrifying screech of tortured metal, and Jim, clinging desperately to the mesh of the pig net, rose slowly and majestically into the air, whirling slowly round and round.

"I wonder if he gets net-sick as well as sea-sick?" said Jacquie.

"Sure to," said Chris callously. "To the best of my knowledge he gets sea-sick, train-sick, car-sick, plane-sick and home-sick, so I can't see him escaping being net-sick as well."

Jim was now about half-way up, still twisting round and round, his white face peering down at us from between the meshes of the net.

"We're all *mad*," we heard him yell above the sound of

the sea and the infernal noise the crane was making. He was still yelling presumably insulting remarks at us when the net disappeared over the edge of the cliff. After a pause it reappeared again and was lowered to the deck, where Chris stepped stoically into it. He stuck his nose and the lens of the camera through the mesh of the net and started to film the moment he was lifted from the deck. Higher and higher he rose, still filming, and then suddenly, when he was poised half-way between the launch and the top of the cliff, the net came to a sudden halt. We watched anxiously but nothing happened for about five minutes, except that Chris continued to go round and round in ever diminishing circles.

"What d'you think has happened?" asked Jacquie.

"I don't know. Perhaps Jim's jammed the crane to get his own back on Chris."

Just as I said this the crane started up again and Chris continued his majestic flight through the air and disappeared over the cliff edge. We discovered later that Jim had set up his camera and tripod in such a position that Alan Wright could not swing the crane in, but Alan was under the impression that Jim had to be in that particular position, so he kept Chris dangling in mid-air. It was only when he saw Jim leave the camera, find a convenient rock and, squatting on it, take out a bar of chocolate and start to eat it, that he realised that he had been keeping Chris dangling like a pantomime fairy to no good purpose, so the camera and tripod were removed and Chris was swung in, demanding vociferously to know why he had been kept suspended in mid-air for so long.

The net was sent down once again, loaded up with our gear, and Jacquie and I reluctantly took our seats.

"I am not going to like this a bit," said Jacquie with conviction.

"Well, if you get scared just close your eyes."

"It's not the height so much," she said, glancing upwards, "it's the strength of that hawser that worries me."

"Oh, I wouldn't worry about *that*," I said cheerfully. "I expect it's been carrying loads like this for years."

"That's exactly what I mean," she said grimly.

"Well, it's too late now," I said philosophically, as the crane started its banshee-like screech and we zoomed up from the deck of the launch at the speed of an express lift. The wide mesh of the net gave you the unpleasant impression that you had been rocketed into the air without any support at all, and as you revolved round and round you could see the waves breaking on the jagged rocks below. The launch now looked like a toy and, glancing up, the top of the cliff appeared to be a good deal higher than Everest, but at last we reached the cliff edge and were swung in and dumped unceremoniously on the ground.

As we disentangled ourselves from the net and equipment, a stocky man who had been operating the crane came forward and shook hands. He had a freckled face, vivid blue eyes and bright red hair.

"I'm Alan Wright," he said. "Pleased to meet you."

"There were moments," I said, glancing at the crane, "when I began to wonder if we should ever meet."

"Oh, she's all right," said Alan, laughing, "she just maithers a bit when she's got a load on, that's all."

We got the equipment up the final slope to the lighthouse on a sort of elongated trolley, drawn up the hillside by a cable and winch. The others decided to walk up but I thought it would be fun to ride up on the trolley and so I perched myself on the camera gear. We were half-way up when I glanced back and suddenly realized that—potentially speaking—this was every bit as dangerous as the trip in the net, for if the hawser that was hauling the truck broke, the truck, weighted down with equipment and myself, would run backwards down the rails and shoot off the edge of the cliff like a rocket. I was glad when we ground to a halt by the lighthouse.

When we had got the gear safely installed in the one

wooden hut which we would all have to share as bed-room and work-shop, I turned to Alan eagerly.

"Tell me," I said, "did you manage to get a Tuatara for us?"

"Oh, aye," he said casually, "that's all right."

"Wonderful," I said enthusiastically. "Can I see it?"

Alan gave me an amused look.

"Aye," he said. "Come with me."

He led Jacquie, Chris and myself to a small shed that stood not far from the hut we were to occupy, unlocked the door and threw it open; we all peered inside.

I have, at one time and another, had many zoological surprises, but, offhand, I can never remember being quite so taken aback as when I peered into that tiny shed on the Brothers. Instead of the one Tuatara I had expected, the whole floor was—quite literally—covered with them. They ranged from great-grandfathers some two feet long to babies measuring some six inches. Alan, glancing at my face, misinterpreted my expression of disbelieving delight for one of horror.

"I hope I haven't got too many," he said anxiously. "Only you didn't say what size you wanted or how many, so I thought I'd better catch you a fair selection."

"My dear fellow," I said in a hushed whisper, "you couldn't have done anything to please me more. There was I, thinking we might be lucky if we just saw *one* Tuatara, and here you provide me with a positive sea of them. It's incredible. Did they take you long to catch?"

"Oh, no," said Alan, "I got this lot last night. I left it until the last minute because I didn't want to keep them shut up too long. But I think there'll be enough for your film, won't there?"

"How many have you got in there?" asked Chris.

"About thirty," said Alan.

"Yes . . . well, I think we can just about scrape through with a mere thirty," said Chris with magnificent con-descension.

We returned to the lighthouse in a jubilant frame of

mind and had an excellent lunch. Then we went back to the shed full of Tuataras and started to choose our stars. Crouching there in the gloom, surrounded by an interested audience of Tuataras, was a fascinating experience. All the young ones were a uniform chocolate brown, a protective coloration which they maintain until they are fully grown, but it was the coloration of the adults that amazed me. Previously the Tuataras I had seen had been unfortunate individuals incarcerated in Reptile Houses in various zoos, where the temperature was kept at a constant eighty or eighty-five degrees—a temperature which is not only totally unsuitable for the unfortunate creature, but which makes it turn a dirty brown out of sheer misery. But these wild-caught adult specimens were how a Tuatara should look, and I thought they looked beautiful. The ground colour of the skin is a sort of greenish-brown, heavily flecked with sage green and sulphur-yellow spots and streaks; both male and female develop crests down their backs, but in the male the crest is larger and more prominent. The crests consist of little triangular bits of white skin of the consistency of thickish paper, that run down from the back of the head to the base of the tail. The tail itself is decorated with a series of hard spikes of the same shape, but whereas the spikes on the tail are the same colour as the tail, the crest along the back is so white it looks as though it has been freshly laundered. The males had massive, regal-looking heads and huge dark eyes, so large that they resembled the eyes of an owl more than anything. After a lot of deliberation we chose one magnificent male, one young one, and a rather pert-looking and well-marked female. The rest of the horde we left carefully locked up in the hut: firstly because we could not release them until nightfall, and secondly, should one of our "stars" escape during the course of the filming, we had a hut full of doubles to fall back on. But we had no difficulty like this, for every Tuatara behaved perfectly in front of the cameras and did exactly what we wanted.

Now, although to the uninitiated eye the Tuatara looks like nothing more nor less than a rather large and majestic lizard, one of the reasons that it makes naturalists like myself foam at the mouth with enthusiasm is that it is not a lizard at all. It is, in fact, so unlike the lizards in its structure that a special new order had to be created for it when it was discovered, an order called the *Rhyncho-cephalia,* which simply means "beak head". Not only did it have the distinction of having a special order created for it, but it was soon discovered that the Tuatara is a genuine, living, breathing prehistoric monster. It is the last survivor of a once widely spread group that was found in Asia, Africa, North America and even Europe. Most of the skeletons that have been found date from the Triassic period of some two hundred million years ago, and they show how alike the "beak heads" of those days were to the present-day Tuatara; to have come down through all those years unchanged surely makes the Tuatara the conservative to end all conservatives. The other thing about this lovely animal that has captured the imagination is the fact that it has a third "eye"—the pineal eye—situated on top of the head midway between the two real eyes, and a lot of unnecessary fuss has been made over this, for Tuataras are not unique in having a pineal eye; several kinds of lizard and some other animals have it as well. The young Tuatara, when it is hatched, has a curious "beak" on the end of its nose (for tearing its way out of the parchment-like shell) and the pineal eye is clearly visible on top of the head. It is an uncovered spot with scales round it, radiating like the petals of a flower. This eye gradually becomes overgrown with scales and in the adult specimens it is impossible to see it. Many experiments to see whether the eye could, in fact, be of any use to the Tuatara have been tried: beams of various wave-lengths have been trained on it and experiments to see whether the eye is possibly receptive to heat have all proved negative in their results. So the Tuatara just ambles through life with its three eyes, a puzzle to biologists and a joy to those naturalists who are fortunate enough to see it. At one time these creatures were found on the mainland of New Zealand, but they have long since been exterminated there, and now they only survive in limited numbers on a few islands (like the Brothers) scattered around the coast, where they—quite rightly—enjoy full protection from the New Zealand Government.

By the time we had finished filming it was sunset, and we suddenly became aware that the Brothers were not just semi-barren humps of rock populated entirely by lighthouse keepers and Tuataras. Fairy Penguins appeared in small groups and hopped their way up the rocks towards their nest burrows, pausing every now and then to throw back their heads and utter a loud, braying cry reminiscent of a small but extremely enthusiastic donkey. Then the Fairy Prions—delicate little swallow-like petrels—started to arrive. It is with the Fairy Prions that the Tuataras have worked out an amicable housing arrangement: the Prion digs a burrow for the reception of its eggs and the Tuataras move in and live with the Prions in what appears to be perfect harmony. This is principally because the Prions are out at sea, fishing, during most of the day, and so only really make use of the burrow at night—at least when they are not incubating. The Tuataras, on the other hand, come out at night in their hunt for beetles, crickets and other provender, so, as the day shift of Prions is winging its way back in the evening light, the Tuatara night shift is just leaving. It seems an admirable but curious relationship; the Tuataras are perfectly capable of digging their own burrows (and in many cases do), but the Prions seem to offer no objection to the Tuataras invading their nests. Whether the Tuataras are ever ungrateful enough to eat the eggs or young of the Prions is a moot point, but it would not be altogether surprising, for reptiles, by and large, have little conscience.

As the sun touched the horizon the Fairy Penguins

started to come ashore in droves, and the Prions glided in like pale ghosts to settle among the low undergrowth and then shuffle awkwardly, in a swift-like manner, down their nesting burrows. As soon as they had disappeared underground they would start talking to each other in a series of loud, purring grunts, squeaks and pigeon-like cooings. As the nest burrows were fairly close together, one could hear twenty or thirty conversations going on at the same time and this, combined with the braying of the penguins, made the whole island literally shake. The nearer ones were, of course, the loudest, but by attuning your ear you discovered that the whole island was vibrating like a gigantic harp with this constant underground chorus.

At length the sun dipped below the sea, the sky turned blood red and then faded rapidly into darkness full of stars, and the yellow, vigilant beam of the lighthouse started to revolve slowly round and round. Presently, full of food, tired, but contented with our day's work, we picked our way down to our hut. While the others were sorting out who was going to sleep where, I took the torch and walked along the cliff edge. The Prions and Penguins were still calling with undiminished enthusiasm and then suddenly, in my torch beam, I saw a Tuatara. He was a huge male, his white frill standing up stiffly along his back, his heavy head raised as he gazed at me with his enormous eyes. After having spotted him I switched off the torch, for the moonlight was quite bright enough for me to watch him. He remained stationary for a few minutes and then started to walk very slowly, and with great dignity, through the undergrowth. All around me the ground shook with the twittering, braying, squeaking and snoring of the birds and the Tuatara strolled majestically through his moonlit kingdom like a dragon. Presently he paused again, looking at me haughtily—but the effect was spoilt, for nature has designed his mouth in a half smile—and then disappeared into the undergrowth.

I wandered sleepily back to the hut and found all the others curled up in their camp beds.

"Ah!" said Jim, poking his head out from what appeared to be a pile of some twenty blankets, "you're interested in birds, aren't you, Gerry? Well, you'll be delighted to know that there are a couple of penguins who've got a semi-detached right under the floor of this hut."

He had hardly finished speaking before the most raucous braying started up immediately beneath my feet. It was so loud it made speech impossible and, if we had not been so tired it would have made sleep impossible, for the penguins sang part songs at five-minute intervals throughout the night, but, I reflected as I jammed a pillow over my head, it had been worth it just to see that one Tuatara moving with such superb nonchalance through the undergrowth of this, his own island.

Moti Guj—Mutineer

RUDYARD KIPLING

Once upon a time there was a coffee-planter in India who wished to clear some forest land for coffee-planting. When he had cut down all the trees and burned the under-wood the stumps still remained. Dynamite is expensive and slow-fire slow. The happy medium for stump-clearing is the lord of all beasts, who is the elephant. He will either push the stump out of the ground with his tusks, if he has any, or drag it out with ropes. The planter, therefore, hired elephants by ones and twos and threes, and fell to work. The very best of all the elephants belonged to the very worst of all the drivers or mahouts; and the superior beast's name was Moti Guj. He was the absolute property of his mahout, which would never have been the case under native rule, for Moti Guj was a creature to be desired by kings; and his name, being translated, meant the Pearl Elephant. Because the British Government was in the land, Deesa, the mahout, enjoyed his property undisturbed. He was dissipated. When he had made much money through the strength of his elephant, he would get extremely drunk and give Moti Guj a beating with a tent-peg over the tender nails of the forefeet. Moti Guj never trampled the life out of Deesa on these occasions, for he knew that after the beating was over Deesa would embrace his trunk, and weep and call him his love and his life and the liver of his soul, and give him some liquor. Moti Guj was very fond of liquor—arrack for choice, though he would drink palm-tree toddy if nothing better offered. Then Deesa would go to sleep between Moti Guj's forefeet, and as Deesa generally chose the middle of the public road, and as Moti Guj mounted guard over him and would not permit horse, foot, or cart to pass by, traffic was congested till Deesa saw fit to wake up.

There was no sleeping in the daytime on the planter's clearing: the wages were too high to risk. Deesa sat on Moti Guj's neck and gave him orders, while Moti Guj rooted up the stumps—for he owned a magnificent pair of shoulders, while Deesa kicked him behind the ears and said he was the king of elephants. At evening time Moti Guj would wash down his three hundred pounds' weight of green food with a quart of arrack, and Deesa would take a share and sing songs between Moti Guj's legs till it was time to go to bed. Once a week Deesa led Moti Guj down to the river, and Moti Guj lay on his side luxuriously in the shallows, while Deesa went over him with a coir-swab and a brick. Moti Guj never mistook the pounding blow of the latter for the smack of the former that warned him to get up and turn over on the other side. Then Deesa would look at his feet, and examine his eyes, and turn up the fringes of his mighty ears in case of sores or budding ophthalmia. After inspection, the two would "come up with a song from the sea", Moti Guj all black and shining, waving a torn tree branch twelve feet long in his trunk, and Deesa knotting up his own long wet hair.

It was a peaceful, well-paid life till Deesa felt the return of the desire to drink deep. He wished for an orgy. The little draughts that led nowhere were taking the manhood out of him.

He went to the planter, and "My mother's dead," said he, weeping.

"She died on the last plantation two months ago; and she died once before that when you were working for me last year," said the planter, who knew something of the way of nativedom.

"Then it's my aunt, and she was just the same as a

mother to me," said Deesa, weeping more than ever. "She has left eighteen small children entirely without bread, and it is I who must fill their little stomachs," said Deesa, beating his head on the floor.

"Who brought you the news?" said the planter.

"The post," said Deesa.

"There hasn't been a post here for the past week. Get back to your lines!"

"A devastating sickness has fallen on my village, and all my wives are dying," yelled Deesa, really in tears this time.

"Call Chihun, who comes from Deesa's village," said the planter. "Chihun, has this man a wife?"

"He!" said Chihun. "No. Not a woman of our village would look at him. They'd sooner marry the elephant." Chihun snorted. Deesa wept and bellowed.

"You will get into a difficulty in a minute," said the planter. "Go back to your work!"

"Now I will speak Heaven's truth," gulped Deesa, with an inspiration. "I haven't been drunk for two months. I desire to depart in order to get properly drunk afar off and distant from this heavenly plantation. Thus I shall cause no trouble."

A flickering smile crossed the planter's face. "Deesa," said he, "you've spoken the truth, and I'd give you leave on the spot if anything could be done with Moti Guj while you're away. You know that he will only obey your orders."

"May the Light of the Heavens live forty thousand years. I shall be absent but ten little days. After that, upon my faith and honour and soul, I return. As to the inconsiderable interval, have I the gracious permission of the Heaven-born to call up Moti Guj?"

Permission was granted, and, in answer to Deesa's shrill yell, the lordly tusker swung out of the shade of a clump of trees where he had been squirting dust over himself till his master should return.

"Light of my heart, Protector of the Drunken, Mountain of Might, give ear," said Deesa, standing in front of him.

Moti Guj gave ear, and saluted with his trunk. "I am going away," said Deesa.

Moti Guj's eyes twinkled. He liked jaunts as well as his master. One could snatch all manner of nice things from the roadside then.

"But you, you fubsy old pig, must stay behind and work."

The twinkle died out as Moti Guj tried to look delighted. He hated stump-hauling on the plantation. It hurt his teeth.

"I shall be gone for ten days, oh Delectable One. Hold up your near forefoot and I'll impress the fact upon it, warty toad of a dried mud-puddle." Deesa took a tent-peg and banged Moti Guj ten times on the nails. Moti Guj grunted and shuffled from foot to foot.

"Ten days," said Deesa, "you must work and haul and root trees as Chihun here shall order you. Take up Chihun and set him on your neck!" Moti Guj curled the tip of his trunk, Chihun put his foot there and was swung on to the neck. Deesa handed Chihun the heavy *ankus*, the iron elephant-goad.

Chihun thumped Moti Guj's bald head as a paviour thumps a kerbstone.

Moti Guj trumpeted.

"Be still, hog of the backwoods. Chihun's your mahout for ten days. And now bid me good-bye, beast after mine own heart. Oh, my lord, my king! Jewel of all created elephants, lily of the herd, preserve your honoured health; be virtuous. Adieu!"

Moti Guj lapped his trunk round Deesa and swung him into the air twice. That was his way of bidding the man good-bye.

"He'll work now," said Deesa to the planter. "Have I leave to go?"

The planter nodded, and Deesa dived into the woods. Moti Guj went back to haul stumps.

Chihun was very kind to him, but he felt unhappy and forlorn notwithstanding. Chihun gave him balls of spices, and tickled him under the chin, and Chihun's little baby cooed to him after work was over, and Chihun's wife called him a darling; but Moti Guj was a bachelor by instinct, as Deesa was. He did not understand the domestic emotions. He wanted the light of his universe back again—the drink and the drunken slumber, the savage beatings and the savage caresses.

None the less he worked well, and the planter wondered. Deesa had vagabonded along the roads till he met a marriage procession of his own caste and, drinking, dancing, and tippling, had drifted past all knowledge of the lapse of time.

The morning of the eleventh day dawned, and there returned no Deesa. Moti Guj was loosed from his ropes for the daily stint. He swung clear, looked round, shrugged his shoulders, and began to walk away, as one having business elsewhere.

"Hi! Ho! Come back you," shouted Chihun. "Come back, and put me on your neck, Misborn Mountain. Return, Splendour of the Hillsides. Adornment of all India, heave to, or I'll bang every toe off your fat forefoot!"

Moti Guj gurgled gently, but did not obey. Chihun ran after him with a rope and caught him up. Moti Guj put his ears forward, and Chihun knew what that meant, though he tried to carry it off with high words.

"None of your nonsense with me," said he. "To your pickets, Devil-son."

"Hrrump!" said Moti Guj, and that was all—that and the forebent ears.

Moti Guj put his hands in his pockets, chewed a branch for a toothpick, and strolled about the clearing, making jest of the other elephants, who had just set to work.

Chihun reported the state of affairs to the planter, who came out with a dog-whip and cracked it furiously. Moti Guj paid the white man the compliment of charging him nearly a quarter of a mile across the clearing and "Hrrumphing" him into the verandah. Then he stood outside the house chuckling to himself, and shaking all over with the fun of it, as an elephant will.

"We'll thrash him," said the planter. "He shall have the finest thrashing that ever elephant received. Give Kala Nag and Nazim twelve foot of chain apiece, and tell them to lay on twenty blows."

Kala Nag—which means Black Snake—and Nazim were two of the biggest elephants in the lines, and one of their duties was to administer the graver punishments, since no man can beat an elephant properly.

They took the whipping-chains and rattled them in their trunks as they sidled up to Moti Guj, meaning to hustle him between them. Moti Guj had never, in all his life of thirty-nine years, been whipped, and he did not intend to open new experiences. So he waited, weaving his head from right to left, and measuring the precise spot in Kala Nag's fat side where a blunt tusk would sink deepest. Kala Nag had no tusks; the chain was his badge of authority; but he judged it good to swing wide of Moti Guj at the last minute, and seem to appear as if he had brought out the chain for amusement. Nazim turned round and went home early. He did not feel fighting-fit that morning, and so Moti Guj was left standing alone with his ears cocked.

That decided the planter to argue no more, and Moti Guj rolled back to his inspection of the clearing. An elephant who will not work, and is not tied up, is not quite so manageable as an eighty-one ton gun loose in a heavy sea-way. He slapped old friends on the back and asked them if the stumps were coming away easily; he talked nonsense concerning labour and the inalienable rights of elephants to a long "nooning" and, wandering to and fro, thoroughly demoralized the garden till sundown, when he returned to his pickets for food.

"If you won't work you shan't eat," said Chihun

angrily. "You're a wild elephant, and no educated animal at all. Go back to your jungle."

Chihun's little brown baby, rolling on the floor of the hut, stretched its fat arms to the huge shadow in the doorway. Moti Guj knew well that it was the dearest thing on earth to Chihun. He swung out his trunk with a fascinating crook at the end, and the brown baby threw itself shouting upon it. Moti Guj made fast and pulled up till the brown baby was crowing in the air twelve feet above his father's head.

"Great Chief!" said Chihun. "Flour cakes of the best, twelve in number, two feet across, and soaked in rum shall be yours on the instant, and two hundred pounds' weight of fresh-cut young sugar-cane therewith. Deign only to put down safely that insignificant brat who is my heart and my life to me."

Moti Guj tucked the brown baby comfortably between his forefeet, that could have knocked into tooth-picks all Chihun's hut, and waited for his food. He ate it, and the brown baby crawled away. Moti Guj dozed, and thought of Deesa. One of many mysteries connected with the elephant is that his huge body needs less sleep than anything else that lives. Four or five hours in the night suffice—two just before midnight, lying down on one side; two just after one o'clock, lying down on the other. The rest of the silent hours are filled with eating and fidgeting and long grumbling soliloquies.

At midnight, therefore, Moti Guj strode out of his pickets, for a thought had come to him that Deesa might be lying drunk somewhere in the dark forest with none to look after him. So all that night he chased through the undergrowth, blowing and trumpeting and shaking his ears. He went down to the river and blared across the shallows where Deesa used to wash him, but there was no answer. He could not find Deesa, but he disturbed all the elephants in the lines, and nearly frightened to death some gipsies in the woods.

At dawn Deesa returned to the plantation. He had been

very drunk indeed, and he expected to fall into trouble for outstaying his leave. He drew a long breath when he saw that the bungalow and the plantation were still uninjured; for he knew something of Moti Guj's temper; and reported himself with many lies and salaams. Moti Guj had gone to his pickets for breakfast. His night exercise had made him hungry.

"Call up your beast," said the planter, and Deesa shouted in the mysterious elephant-language, that some mahouts believe came from China at the birth of the world, when elephants and not men were masters. Moti Guj heard and came. Elephants do not gallop. They move from spots at varying rates of speed. If any elephant wished to catch an express train he could not gallop, but he could catch the train. Thus Moti Guj was at the planter's door almost before Chihun noticed that he had left his pickets. He fell into Deesa's arms trumpeting with joy, and the man and beast wept and slobbered over each other, and handled each other from head to heel to see that no harm had befallen.

"Now we will get to work," said Deesa. "Lift me up, my son and my joy."

Moti Guj swung him up and the two went to the coffee-clearing to look for irksome stumps.

The planter was too astonished to be very angry.

Under The Ice-roof

CHARLES G. D. ROBERTS

I

Filtering thinly down through the roof of snow and clean blue ice, the sharp winter sunshine made almost a summer's glow upon the brown bottom of the pond. Beneath the ice the water was almost as warm now as in summer, the pond being fed by springs from so deep a source that their temperature hardly varied with the seasons. Here and there a bit of water-weed stood up from the bottom, green as in June. But in the upper world, meanwhile, the wind that drove over the ice and snow was so intensely cold that the hardy northern trees snapped under it, and few of the hardy northern creatures of the wilderness, though fierce with hunger, had the fortitude to face it. They crouched shivering in their lairs, under fallen trunks or in the heart of dense fir thickets, and waited anxiously for the rigour of cold and the savagery of wind to abate. Only down in the pond, in the generous spaces of amber water beneath the ice-roof, life went on busily and securely. The wind might rage unbridled, the cold might lay its hand of death heavily on forest and hill; but the beavers in their unseen retreat knew nothing of it. All it could do was to add an inch or two of thickness to the icy shelter above them, making their peaceful security more secure.

The pond was a large one, several acres in extent, with a depth of fully five feet in the deeper central portions, which were spacious enough to give the beavers room for play and exercise. Around the shallow edges the ice, which was fully fifteen inches thick beneath its blanket of snow, lay solid on the bottom.

The beavers of this pond occupied a lodge on the edge of the deep water, not far above the dam. This lodge was a broad-based, low-domed house of mud, turf, and sticks cunningly interwoven, and rising about four feet above the surface of the ice-roof. The dome, though covered deep with snow, was conspicuous to every prowler of the woods, who would come at times to sniff greedily at the warm smell of beaver steaming up from the minute air-vents in the apex. But however greedy, however ravenous, the prowling vagrants might be, the little dome-builders and dam-builders within neither knew nor cared about their greed, the dome was fully two feet thick, built solidly, and frozen almost to the hardness of granite. There were no claws among all the ravening forest kindred strong enough to tear their way through such defences. In the heart of the lodge, in a dry grass-lined chamber just above high-water level, the beavers dwelt warm and safe.

But it was not from the scourge of the northern cold alone, and the ferocity of their enemies, that the beavers were protected by their ice-roof and their frozen dome. The winter's famine, too, they had well guarded them-selves against. Before the coming of the frost, they had gnawed down great quantities of birch, poplar, and wil-low, cut them into convenient, manageable lengths, and dragged them to a spot a little above the centre of the dam, where the water was deepest. Here the store of logs, poles, and brush made a tangled mass from the bottom up to the ice. When it was feeding-time in the hidden chamber of the lodge, a beaver would swim to the brush pile, pull out a suitable stick, and drag it into the chamber. Here the family would feast at their ease, in the dry, pungent gloom, eating the bark and the delicate outer layer of young wood. When the stick was stripped clean,

111

another beaver would drag it out and tow it down to the dam, there to await its final use as material for repairs. Every member of the colony was blest with a good appetite, and there was nearly always at least one beaver to be seen swimming through the amber gloom, either with a green stick from the brush pile, or a white stripped one to deposit on the base of the dam.

For these most diligent of all the four-foot kindreds this was holiday time. Under the ice-roof they had no dam-building, no tree-cutting, no house-repairing. There was nothing to do but eat, sleep, and play. There was not much variety to their play, to be sure; but the monotony of it did not trouble them. Sometimes two would indulge in a sort of mad game of tag, swimming at marvellous speed close beneath the ice, their powerful hind legs propelling them, their tiny little fore paws held up demurely under their chins, and their broad, flat, hairless tails stretched straight out behind to act as rudders. As they swam this way and that, they loosed a trail of silvery bubbles behind them, from the air carried under their close fur. At last one of the players, unable to hold his breath any longer, would whisk sharply into the mouth of the black tunnel leading into the lodge, scurry up into the chamber, and lie there panting, to be joined a moment later by his equally breathless pursuer. One by one the other members of the colony would dip in, till the low chamber was full of furry, snuggling warmth and well-fed content. Little cared the beavers whether it was night or day in the wide, frozen, perilous world above the ice-roof, whether the sun shone from the bitter blue, or the wolf-haunted moonlight lay upon the snow, or the madness of the blizzard made the woods cower before its fury.

As long as the cold endured and the snow lay deep upon the wilderness, the beavers lived their happy, uneventful life beneath the ice-roof. But in this particular winter the untempered cold of December and January, which slew many of the wood folk and drove the others wild with hunger, broke suddenly in an unprecedented thaw. Not the oldest bear of the Bald Mountain caves could remember any such thaw. First there were days on days, and nights on nights, of bland, melting rain, softer than April's. The snow vanished swiftly from the laden branches of fir and spruce and hemlock, and the silent woods stood up black and terrible against the weeping sky. On the ground and on the ice of pond and stream the snow shrank, settled, and assumed a greyish complexion. Water, presently, gathered in great spreading, leaden-coloured pools on the ice; and on the naked knolls the bare moss and petty shrubs began to emerge. Every narrow watercourse soon carried two streams,—the temperate, fettered, summer-mindful stream below the ice, and the swollen, turbulent flood above. Then the rain stopped. The sun came out warm and urgent as in latter May. And snow and ice together dwindled under the unnatural caress.

The beavers, in their safe seclusion, had knowledge in two ways of this strange visitation upon the world. Not all the soft flood of the melting snow ran over the surface of their ice, but a portion got beneath it, by way of the upper brooks. This extra flow disturbed both the colour and the temperature of the clear amber water of the pond. It lifted heavily against the ice, pressed up the tunnels to the very edge of the dry chamber of the lodge, and thrust ponderously at the outlets of the dam. Understanding the peril, the wise little dam-builders sallied forth in a flurry, and with skilful tooth and claw lost no time in enlarging the outlets. They were much too intelligent to let the flood escape by a single outlet, lest the concentrated flow should become too heavy for them to control it. They knew the spirit of that ancient maxim of tyrants, *"divide et impera"*. By dividing the overflow into many feeble streams they knew how to rule it. This done, they rested in no great anxiety, expecting the thaw to end with a stringent frost.

Then, however, came the second, and more significant, manifestation of peril. The snow on the ice-roof had vanished; and looking up through the ice they saw the flood eddying riotously over the naked expanse. It was a portent which the wiser elders understood. The whole colony fell to work strengthening the dam where the weight of the current bore down upon it, and increasing the outlet along the farther edges.

A thaw so persistent, however, and at the same time so violent, overpassed their cunning calculations. One night, when all had done their best and, weary, but reassured, had withdrawn into the warm chamber of the lodge, something happened that they had never looked for. In their snug retreat they were falling to sleep, the rush of the overflow and the high clamour of the side vents coming dimly to their ears, when suddenly they were startled by the water being forced up over the dry floor of the chamber. The pressure of water beneath the ice had suddenly increased. They were more than startled. They were badly frightened. If the water should rise much higher they would be drowned helplessly, for the ice lay close all over the pond. The younger ones scurried this way and that with plaintive squeaks, and several dashed forth into the pond in a panic, forgetting that there was no escape in that direction. A moment later a low crashing penetrated to the dark chamber; and the invading water retreated down the tunnel. The ice-roof, worn thin, honeycombed, and upheaved by the pressure from below, had gone to pieces.

It was the older and wiser beavers who had remained in the chamber, terrified, but not panic-stricken. When the water retreated to its normal level—about two inches below the chamber floor—they were satisfied. Then, however, a louder and heavier note in the rush of the overflow came to their ears, and their anxiety returned with fresh force. Thrusting their whiskered noses inquiringly down the tunnel, they observed that the water was sinking far below its proper level. Well they knew what that meant. The dam was broken. The water, which was their one protection from the terrors of the forest, was escaping.

This was the kind of an emergency which a beaver will always rise to. Shy as they are, under ordinary circumstances, when the dam is attacked their courage is unfailing. In a moment every beaver in the colony was out among the swirling ice, under the broad, white moonlight which they had not seen for so long.

It was at its very centre, where the channel was deepest and the thrust of the water most violent, that the dam had given way. The break was about ten feet wide, and not, as yet, of any great depth. It was the comparatively narrow and unsubstantial crust of the embankment which had yielded, disintegrated by the thaw and ripped by the broken edges of the ice.

The vehemence of the torrent was rapidly cutting down into the firmer body of the dam, when the beavers flung themselves valiantly into the breach. In the face of the common danger they forgot all caution, and gave no heed to any hungry eyes that might be glaring at them from the woods on either shore. Without any apparent leadership in the work, they all seemed to help each other in whatever way would be most effective. Some dragged up the longest and heaviest poles from the pile of stripped stuff, floated them carefully into the break, butt end up-stream and parallel with the flow, and held them there doggedly with their teeth and fore paws till others could come with more timbers to hold the first lot down. Meanwhile, from the soft bottom along the base of the dam, big lumps of mingled clay and grass-roots, together with small stones to add weight, were grabbed up and heaped solidly upon the layers of sticks for anchorage. This loose stuff, though deposited along the upper ends of the sticks where the flow was least violent, and swiftly packed down into the interstices, was mostly washed away in the process. It was seemingly an even struggle, for a time, and the beavers could do no more than hold the breach from deepening and widening. But they were quite undaunted; and they seemed to know no such thing as fatigue. Little by little they gained upon the torrent, making good the hold of a mass of turf here, a few stones there, and everywhere the long straight sticks upon which the water could get but slight grip. The flood grew shallower and less destructive. More sticks were brought, more stones, and clay, and grass-roots; and then a layer of heavy, clean poles, over which the water slid thinly and smoothly without danger to the structure beneath.

The dam was now strongest at this point, its crest being broader and formed of heavier timbers than elsewhere. But no sooner had the hard-won victory been secured, and the plucky little architects paused for breath, than there came an ominous crackling from far over to the extreme left of the dam, where a subsidiary channel had offered a new vantage to the baffled torrent. The crackling was mingled with a loud rushing noise. Another section of the crest of the dam had been swept away. A white curtain of foam sprang into the moonlight, against the darkness of the trees.

II

While the brave little dam-builders had been battling with the flood, out there in the wide-washing moonlight, hungry eyes had been watching them from the heart of a dense spruce thicket, a little below the left end of the dam. The watching had been hopeless enough, as the owner of those fierce, narrow eyes knew it was no use trying to surprise a beaver in the open, when the whole pond was right there for him to dive into. But now when the new break brought the whole colony swimming madly to the left-hand shore, and close to the darkness of the woods, those watching eyes glowed with a savage expectancy, and began slowly, noiselessly, steadily, floating nearer through the undisturbed underbrush.

The tremendous thaw, loosing the springs and streams on the high flanks of Bald Mountain, had washed out the snow from the mouth of a shallow cave and rudely aroused a young bear from his winter sleep. As soon as he had shaken off his heaviness the bear found himself hungry. But his hunting thus far had not been successful. His training had not been in the winter woods. He hardly knew what to look for, and the soft slumping snow hampered him. One panic-stricken white rabbit, and a few ants from a rotten stump, were all that he had found to eat in three days. His white fangs in his red jaws had slavered with craving as he watched the plump beavers at their work, far out on the brightly moonlit dam. When, at last, they came hurrying towards him, and fell to work on the new break within thirty or forty yards of his hiding-place, he could hardly contain himself. He did contain himself, however; for he had hunted beaver before, and not with a success to make him over-confident. Right by the termination of the dam, where the beavers were working, the woods came down thick and dark to within eight or ten feet of the water. Towards this point he made his way patiently, and with such control of every muscle that, for all his apparent clumsiness, not a twig snapped, not a branch rustled, any more than if a shadow were gliding through them. He saw one old beaver sitting stiffly erect on the crest of the dam, a wary sentinel, sniffing the still air and scanning the perilous woods; but he planned to make his final rush so swift that the sentinel would have no time to give warning.

But the fierce little eyes of the bear, dark and glinting red, were not the only ones that watched the beavers at their valorous toil. In the juniper scrub, a short distance up the bank of this pond, crouched two big grey lynxes, glaring down upon the scene with wide, round, pale greenish eyes, unspeakably sinister. The lynxes were gaunt with famine. Fired with the savage hope that some chance might bring a beaver within reach of their mighty spring, they had crept down, on their great, furred,

117

stealthy pads, to the patch of juniper scrub. Here they had halted, biding their time with that long, painful patience which is the price of feeding—the price of life—among the winter-scourged kindreds. Now, when the beavers had so considerately come over to the edge of the woods, and appeared to be engrossed in some incomprehensible pulling and splashing and mud-piling, the two lynxes felt that their opportunity had arrived. Their bellies close to the snow, their broad, soft-padded feet stepping lightly as the fall of feathers, their light grey fur all but invisible among the confused moon-shadows, their round, bright eyes unwinking, they seemed almost to drift down through the thickets towards their expected prey.

Neither the bear creeping up from below the dam, nor the two lynxes stealing down from above it, had eyes or thought for anything in the world but the desperately toiling beavers. Their hunger was gnawing at their lean stomachs, the fever of the hunt was in their veins, and the kill was all but within reach. A few moments more, and the rush would come, up from the fir thickets—the long, terrible spring and pounce, down from the juniper scrub.

The work of repairing the breach was making good progress. Already the roaring overflow was coming into subjection, its loud voice dwindling to a shallow clamour. Then, something happened. Perhaps the wary sentinel on the crest of the dam detected a darker shade stirring among the firs, or a lighter greyness moving inexplicably between the bushes up the bank. Perhaps his quick nostrils caught a scent that meant danger. Perhaps the warning came to him mysteriously, flashed upon that inner sense, sometimes alert and sometimes densely slumbering, which the forest furtiveness seems to develop in its creatures. However it came, it came. Dropping forward as if shot, the sentinel beaver brought his flat tail down upon the surface of the water with a smack that rang all up and around the borders of the pond, startling the quiet of the night. In a fraction of a second every beaver had vanished beneath the shining surface.

At the same moment, or an eye-wink later, a strange thing happened—one of those violent surprises with which the vast repression of the forest sometimes betrays itself. Maddened to see his prey escaping, the bear made his rush, launching himself, a black and uncouth mass, right down to the water's edge. Simultaneously the two lynxes shot into the air from higher up the bank, frantic with disappointed hunger. With a screech of fury, and a harsh spitting and snarling, they landed a few feet distant from the bear, and crouched flat, their stub tails twitching, their eyes staring, their tufted ears laid back upon their skulls.

Like a flash the bear wheeled, confronting the two great cats with uplifted paw and mouth wide open. Half-sitting back upon his haunches, he was ready for attack or defence. His little eyes glowed red with rage. To him it was clearly the lynxes who had frightened off the beavers and spoiled his hunting; and interference of this kind is what the wild kindreds will not tolerate. To the lynxes, on the other hand, it was obvious that the bear had caused the whole trouble. He was the clumsy interloper who had come between them and their quarry. They were on the verge of that blindness of fury which might hurl them, at any instant, tooth and claw, upon their formidable foe. For the moment, however, they had not quite lost sight of prudence. The bear was master of the forest, and they knew that even together they two were hardly a match for him.

The bear, on the other hand, was not quite sure that he was willing to pay the price of vengeance. His blood surging in the swollen veins, he growled with heavy menace, and rocking forward upon his haunches he seemed on the point of rushing in. But he knew how those powerful knife-edged claws of the lynxes could rend. He knew that their light bodies were strong and swift and elusive, their teeth almost as punishing as his own. He felt himself the master; nevertheless he realized that it would cost dear to enforce that mastery. He hesi-

119

tated. Had he made the slightest forward move, the lynxes would have thrown caution to the winds, and sprung upon him. On the other hand, had the lynxes even tightened up their sinews to spring, he would have hurled himself with a roar into the battle. But as it was, both sides held themselves in leash, tense, ready, terrible in restraint. And as the moments dragged by, out on the bright surface of the pond small heads appeared, with little bright eyes watching curiously.

For perhaps three or four long, intense minutes there was not a move made. Then the round eyes of the lynxes shifted ever so little, while the bear's eyes never faltered. The bear's was the steadier purpose, the more tenacious and resolute temper. Almost imperceptibly the lynxes shrank backward, gliding inch by inch. A swift side-glance showed them that the way of retreat was open. Then, as if both were propelled by the one vehement impulse, they bounded into the air, one whirling aside and the other almost doubling back upon his own trail. Quicker than it takes to tell it, they were fleeing like grey shadows, one over the bank and through the juniper bushes, the other up along the snowy shore of the pond, their discomfiture apparently driving them to part company. The bear, as if surprised, sat up on his haunches to stare after them. Then, with a hungry look at the beavers, now swimming openly far out in the moonlight, he turned and shambled off to find some more profitable hunting.

For a few minutes all was stillness, save for the rushing of the water over the dam. The solitude of the night had resumed its white and tranquil dominion as if nothing had ever occurred to jar its peace. Then once more the watchful sentinel appeared, sitting erect on the dam, and the diligent builders busied themselves to complete the mending of the breach.

NATUK
Experiences in the life of Dr. H. G. Esmonde

TOLD BY MAJOR GEORGE BRUCE

Most people know something of the North-west Mounted Police. Novels and films have made them familiar with the dashing horsemen in red coats and stetson hats. But not everyone realizes that in the Far North of Canada the dashing horseman does not exist. On rare occasions of ceremony at some big post, one of the Mounted Police might turn out in boots and spurs; but our ordinary work in those latitudes was done in summer by canoe or on foot, in winter by dog-team sledge.

North of Lat. 60° the country could never have been opened up by white men, had it not been for that splendid creature the husky, who is just the timber-wolf, domesticated for ages by the Eskimo and the Indian. Fitted by nature to live under conditions of severest hardship, few animals, if any, can match him in courage and endurance. It is no exaggeration to say that Canada owes more to the husky dog than to any man in her history. And I myself owe my life to the best husky I ever owned.

I was on the Porcupine River, some fifty miles north of Rat Lake, well on the cool side of the Arctic Circle, but just then we were having our short hot summer. The day temperature often rose to 80°, and in the evenings there seemed to be more mosquitoes than fresh air. My cabin stood by a small lake from which a stream ran down to the river, among low hills covered with spruce forest. I spent many hours roaming through that forest, or sitting still, watching the wild life that filled it. Among bracken and brambles, fallen trees and branches, it was easy to find a hiding-place from which one could see all round. There was plenty to see, if a man stayed quiet and kept his eyes open: birds of many sorts, foxes, martens, squirrels, mink, the friendly little chipmunks, perhaps a deer, perhaps a she-wolf with a small cub, a lumbering bear in search of food, or a porcupine stripping the rough outer bark from a sapling spruce, to feed on the succulent inner skin.

One day I had been for a long walk through the woods and was on my way back when I came upon a wolverine trap. It had been sprung, and in it, lying dead, was a beautiful husky bitch. She must have run away from some Indian camp, the call of her wolf ancestors in her blood, and taken to the woods.

The trap had been set for wolves or wolverines, pestilent brutes both, and it was clearly right that I should set it again. I forced down the spring till I could open the powerful spiked jaws, and was pulling out the dead husky when I heard a whimper. Out from under the body crawled a little pup, only a few weeks old. I tucked him into the breast of my coat and re-set the trap, after which I skinned the husky, thinking that her pelt would make a good rug for my cabin, and then started for home.

My dogs were tied up, but when I put the pup down and began to open the cabin door they evidently scented him, and a savage growl arose, a growl that told of their smelling possible food. The pup sensed the danger and huddled close to my feet as I entered the cabin.

I fed him on condensed milk till he was old enough to eat solid food, and at night he would curl into my bunk with me. Before long he would follow me everywhere unless I had to go out for the day, when he would settle down on the rug beside my bed, the rug I had made out of his mother's skin. Evidently he found some friendly influence in it; for while I was away he would lie there quite happy and never move.

After the first week I introduced him formally to the sledge dogs. They sniffed him over, each in turn, and then accepted him as a regular member of the household. Soon he would take all manner of liberties with them, usually borne with amused tolerance, but if he went too far—if, for example, he tugged too vigorously with his sharp little teeth at a big dog's ear—a growl and a warning snap of teeth would follow. The pup would flee in any direction and lie low till the atmosphere cleared, when he would come back and play more gently.

My team leader especially became very attached to the youngster. When I took the sledge out I would put the pup on top of the load, and the team leader soon recognized this as part of the regular routine. Before starting he would look round to see that the pup was on the load. If he was not, no shouts or whip-cracks would induce the leader to start till the pup was duly installed in his proper place.

From the first I decided that he was not to be a sledge dog, but was to be my personal companion; and a splendid companion he proved. He came with me on all my rambles through the woods, and if I was looking for meat he would put up rabbits for me to shoot. I soon trained him not to chase them, and as his intelligence developed I taught him many things. I would leave some article on the doorstep and send him back to fetch it, till he would do so from a long distance. Later I would give him something, a glove or mitten perhaps, sending him home to leave it on the doorstep and return.

Perhaps because he was never treated as harshly as one has to treat sledge dogs, he showed a sensitive nature such as I have known in no other husky. I never once had to beat him; a tap of my fingers on his nose was the utmost correction he needed, and he would look up with a pathetic expression as much as to say, "What have I done wrong?" As a watch-dog he was unsurpassed. No

stranger could approach the cabin unless I introduced
him, when the dog would sniff him all over with a low
throaty growl, and would never fail to know him if he
came again.

By the time he had grown to his full size, a magnificent
dog, we were inseparable companions. He would hardly
let me out of his sight; wherever I went he followed close
at my heels. I called him "Natuk", which in the West
Eskimo language means "Shadow". We lived alone, far
from any human society, and our comradeship grew
closer and closer as time went on, till I used to feel that he
knew exactly what I was thinking about.

A handsome animal was Natuk, about thirty inches at
the shoulder and weighing close on nine stone. His colour was that of a sable collie, but a few shades lighter,
with dark tips to the long hair, especially on his flanks,
while his broad chest was almost white. Probably his sire
was a timber-wolf, for he had the true wolf head with
sharp prick-ears, though a white blaze on his face
suggested a strain of Newfoundland in his dam, which
may have accounted for his weight and strength. His
bushy tail was carried in proper husky style, close-curled
over his back.

My position in the Mounted Police was officially that
of doctor, but in that sparsely populated region the calls
for medical or surgical help were few, and unofficially I
did a good deal of regular police work, especially in the
matter of keeping an eye on any strangers who might
drift into the country, and finding out all about them.
Some fifty miles away lived a friend of mine, a Dogrib
Indian, whom I found very useful in getting me information of this kind, information which I passed on to the
proper quarter.

Early in October a rumour reached me of two new-
comers to the district who did not sound desirable visi-
tors. I decided to look up my Indian friend and see what
he could tell me about them. The first snow had already
fallen, and as usual, before the weather grows really cold,

it was soft and yielding. Snow of that kind makes bad travelling for a dog sledge, and fifty miles being a short journey as we reckon things in the North, I planned to do it on foot, pulling a light toboggan with the few things I needed—rifle, blankets, grub, and a small shelter-tent. Natuk, of course, would come with me, and my Indian chore-boy would look after the sledge dogs till my return.

About twenty-five miles out, half-way to my destination, was the cabin of my nearest neighbour, a Swedish trapper and a good friend of mine. Ole Oleson was a man with more education that the average trapper, and a better philosophy of life. In the spring, when he took his winter's harvest of furs to the trading post, instead of spending the proceeds in a riotous orgy, he would bank most of the money and come back to the North to earn more. He was now a well-to-do man. His cabin was comfortable beyond the ordinary standard; he was intelligent and a good talker, and I always enjoyed an evening with him.

Starting early, Natuk and I made Ole's cabin late in the afternoon. We had a hearty welcome from the trapper, and spent a pleasant evening. Next morning after breakfast I began to pack my gear on the toboggan, when Ole begged me not to go.

"There's a blizzard coming," he said. "Stop here today, and you can go when it has blown over."

Ole was an experienced backwoodsman, but so was I, having been born and brought up in that country. I looked at the sky and could see no sign of an approaching storm.

"I reckon you're wrong, Ole," I said.

"I'm not," said he. "It's sure coming. I can smell it."

I did not believe him, and I said so. I was anxious to push on, as I felt it was important to see the Indian and lay him on to those two strangers before they could start any funny business. But Ole insisted, and the end of it was that we lit our pipes and sat talking and smoking till well after mid-day. Then I decided that I could delay no longer, so I finished packing the toboggan and said—

"Well, Ole, if I *do* get into a jam, I'll send Natuk back to you and he'll guide you to wherever I happen to be."

Natuk and I set out, taking a trail that led through the upper hills where the spruce forest was thin and open. The sun went down about three o'clock, and with its setting a wind sprang up, growing rapidly stronger. I began to think that Ole might be right about the blizzard, and turned downhill towards the thick spruce in the valley, which would give some shelter. I was going as fast as I could when suddenly the ground gave way under my feet, and dropped into space. Throwing out my hands instinctively to save myself, I let go the rope, and the toboggan skidded away among the trees.

In a moment I realised what had happened. I had fallen into an Indian bear-trap, scores of which were to be found in these hills. A wide pit is dug, about eight feet deep, one or more pointed stakes fixed in the bottom, the top crossed by stretchers of young saplings, over which is laid a cover of small branches and brush-wood. The snow had hidden the trap effectively, and I had walked straight into it.

Not having the weight or bulk of a bear, I had not gone to the bottom. I was caught round the waist by a mass of jagged sticks, the upper part of my body free, but on kicking about to try for some foothold I found that the pit was full of brambles and dead twigs that had fallen through the cover. This meant that the trap was an old one, perhaps several years old.

That set me thinking. Probably the stretchers covering the trap were pretty rotten. If I struggled too violently, the whole thing might collapse and land me at the bottom of the pit, where the pointed hardwood stakes might still be sound enough and sharp enough to impale me. Even if they were not, it would be impossible to climb out, and I should starve to death miserably in that tangle of dead sticks and brambles.

Cautiously I tried to work my way out of the raffle of
spiky branches that gripped me, but in vain. I had no
foothold to give me a purchase, and my efforts only
resulted in my sinking a few inches lower. The wind was
blowing a gale now, and I could hear dead trees falling far
and near. Suddenly a sharp crack sounded close by. A
dead spruce, split by the frost of some previous winter,
broke off, the whole top of one half falling across the
bear-trap and pinning me down. I was not much hurt,
but only my right arm remained free; my left arm and my
body were held as in a vice among the network of broken
boughs and débris.

All this time Natuk had been jumping round me,
scratching in the snow, trying to dig me out, and
pulling at sticks with his teeth. Several times he broke
through the top crust, but having four legs he was able to
scramble out. Now that I was helplessly pinioned, it
flashed into my mind that he might really be able to assist
me. I had said in joke to Ole that if I got into a jam I would
send Natuk to fetch him. That joke could be turned into
reality if Natuk was as clever as I believed him to be.

When I came in from a journey I would often get him
to pull off my big moose-hide mittens, and now I called
him, holding out my free right hand till he caught the end
of the mitten in his teeth. As he pulled it off I said, "Take
it back and get help, Natuk!" waving my hand in the
direction of Ole's cabin. Natuk looked at me as if trying
to grasp what I was saying; then, as I repeated the order
and pointed to the way, he seemed to catch the idea. With
one snap he gripped the mitten firmly in his mouth and
set off at a loping wolf-canter on the line that I had given
him.

There I was, left all alone, with plenty of time to think
things over. I began to calculate when I might expect help
to come. We had covered about ten miles when I turned
off the trail. With the wild animal's instinct for short-
cuts, Natuk should bring that down to seven miles at
most, and could do that in an hour. It should not take Ole

more than an hour and a half to harness up his dog-team and come out. So in two hours and a half, three hours at most, I might expect to be released.

The wind dropped as quickly as it had risen, and in an hour's time the air was again perfectly still. Not a sound of any kind in the woods, only the dead silence of an Arctic winter night. Though there was no moon it was by no means dark, as the brilliance of the stars in that clear air, refracted from the snow, gives light enough to see things fairly well at a short distance.

In my constrained position, half lying with my feet unsupported, I grew very stiff and cold, especially my right arm. When the tree fell I had thrown it up to guard my head, with the result that a forked branch had trapped it so that I could not bring my hand lower than my shoulder. Now that the heavy moose-hide mitten was gone, I had no protection for that hand but the woollen inner mitten. Lucky for me that the wind had dropped, or I should have been frost-bitten. Round me was a cage of bare branches; in front of me the long split trunk of the spruce, its flat upper side showing white in the starlight.

Slowly the time crawled on, while I tried to picture my dog racing through the woods to the trapper's cabin; Ole's face when he saw him; the hurried harnessing of the dog-team to the sledge and the Swede dashing along the trail; Natuk, ahead of the team, going all out to bring help to his master and friend.

Then through the profound silence of the winter woods rang a blood-freezing cry, the howl of a lone wolf. There is a difference between the howl of a wolf that leads a pack, on first scenting his quarry, and that of a solitary beast, the ex-leader of a pack, driven from his position by a younger and stronger rival. The difference is not to be described in words, but the lone wolf's howl has an indefinable quality which a trained ear cannot mistake, an aggressive and defiant note, as if voicing the bitterness that rankles in the heart of the deposed leader. That sense of defeat, joined to the craft and cunning which years of leadership have given him, makes the lone wolf the most dangerous beast in all the North.

I could hear that cry now, its low cadence gradually working up to the full-throated howl, then dying away. A long pause, ten minutes at least, and it came again, this time nearer and louder. Once more it sounded, nearer still, and then the deep silence of the night. I listened with every nerve strung. Was it my scent that the hunter had winded, or that of some night-roaming animal?

Near the butt of the fallen spruce I suddenly saw two points of green light. They moved forward, and behind them I could just make out a ghostly form creeping along the tree-trunk. I shouted, and the brute backed away but before long he crept forward again. Again I shouted, and again, and each time he drew back. I kept on shouting till my voice dropped to a hoarse croak. The wolf grew bolder, and came on slowly till he was no more than ten or twelve feet away.

In spite of the peril of my position I could not help feeling the grim humour of it. Here was I, a grown man in full health and strength, at the mercy of a beast not half my size. Born and reared in these northern forests, trained from childhood in all the woodcraft and hunting lore of the Indians, I felt that the rawest tenderfoot could not have got himself into a worse mess. My revolver, a Colt's .45, capable of killing six wolves in ten seconds, hung from my belt fully loaded. But I could not get either hand down to draw it, and the wolf was master of the situation. The thing was just absurd.

Absurd or not, however, I must do what I could while any hope remained. Indian hunters had often told me that a wolf will never attack so long as a man keeps up some rhythmic motion. I began to wave my right hand in a measured swing from side to side, and I could see the wolf's head and eyes following the movement. He stood there half crouched, a lean hungry-looking brute, saliva dripping from his jaws, and those baleful green eyes glowing dimly in the starlight; but he came no nearer. I was numb with cold, and my arm grew so weary with the steady movement that I began to wonder how long I could keep it up. The chill of utter exhaustion was creeping over me. Soon I should be unable to swing my hand any more, and then ...

Three shots rang out—distant, but clear in the still night air. Ole was firing to signal his coming. A rush of hope surged through me, lending a momentary spasm of energy to my weary arm. But the sound of those shots seemed to rouse the wolf from his inaction, as if he felt that his time was short and that he must get to work. With fangs bared he began to creep nearer. My strength was almost gone, another moment and those fangs would be in my throat.

A heavy body hurtled through the air. Natuk, his teeth buried in the wolf's shoulder, flung him off the tree, and the two were locked in a fierce grapple in the hollow of the bear-trap. The snow flew in showers as the fight maddened to fury. Both fought mute after the manner of wolves, not a sound but the snap and slash of teeth and the dull rip of skin and flesh. If ever I prayed in my life, I prayed in those moments that my dog might win.

The duel went on, fierce and deadly, both combatants fighting to kill. If Natuk was a shade the heavier, the wolf was an experienced brute that had fought his way to the head of the pack and kept his position for years by dint of ferocity and fangs. My vision was so cramped and their movements so quick that for a time I could not tell which was getting the better of it.

At length the wolf bounded out of the hollow on to the level ground. Natuk leaped after him, and the death-worry began again. I saw Natuk grip the wolf by the side of the neck and throw him clean over his back. Then I must have fainted, for I knew no more till I heard the crack of a pistol close at hand—Ole finishing off the wolf.

It seemed ages before Ole dragged me clear of the bear-trap. I was too spent to give him any help, and it needed all his great strength to pull me out. My first thought was to look at Natuk. He lay on the blood-soaked snow, hideously mauled, a mass of wounds. Both shoulders were torn to the bone, one ear was slashed off, his flank ripped open to the ribs, and the entrails sagging out. But his eyes spoke to me dumbly, and he tried to lick my hand.

We of the North have not much use for sentiment. Life is too hard and death too near at all times to encourage any soft-hearted emotions, and my bringing-up among the Indians had case-hardened my feelings since child-hood. But the sight of my friend and comrade lying there in such agony brought me nearer to a breakdown than ever before or since. Yet the wolf was in a worse state, and it can hardly have needed Ole's bullet to give the *coup de grâce*. Natuk was dying, but he had won the battle.

I knew too much of wounds to have any hope. The only kindness I could show Natuk was to put him out of his pain. I drew my revolver, but the look in the dog's eyes was too much for me, and I dropped it back into the holster. "Ole," I said, "I'll leave it to you to do him the good turn."

Sick at heart, I crept away among the bushes, pulling my coat over my head, till through the heavy fur I heard a muffled report and knew that all was over. We put Natuk on the sledge, and next day I buried him in a clearing near the trapper's cabin, where the sun would shine upon his grave. At its head I placed a heavy wooden slab, and on it cut three words deeply with my knife—

NATUK MY SHADOW

The Loons of Thunder Bay

H. MORTIMER BATTEN

The parent loons must have been wise old birds for, though they had a bigger nest than any of their neighbours, not one rush nor stick had they themselves contributed to the building of it. All that tiresome business had been left to those who were to become the closest of their neighbours, though admittedly the male loon had shown every eagerness to collect and carry during the brief period that the nesting fever possessed him. He had fished up all manner of slimy rubbish from the lake bottom and at hourly intervals proudly presented it to his wife, who had disdainfully rejected his offering, so eventually he sailed off to the centre of the lake to do a bit of fishing on his own. There he had called back to her repeatedly and listened for her answers, but she was too busy with her own affairs to pay heed to his calling.

As a matter of fact the arrangement regarding their free home worked very well, for the loons were saved a lot of trouble in building a nest for themselves and the true builders were to gain rather than lose. All the loons did was to take possession of the domed top of a muskrat house by the shore as soon as it was ready, and the female loon trampled out a hollow to take her eggs on the top of the huge pile of dead sedges and willow wands—exactly the materials they themselves would have chosen. Fully a week's work was thus saved, and they actually had a better nest than the slovenly affair they might have built

132

for themselves for it stood in deep water with foundations as firm as the Bank of Canada.

Immediately under the roof on which the loons were sit the rats had gnawed out their drying-room and nursery, nicely above the interior water level. Their method had been to build the pile first and then, starting at the bottom where it rested on the lake bed, they had gnawed a single passage slanting up into the dome. There they had made the two living chambers, separated by a strong partition, with the underwater passage as their only entrance and exit.

The roof was eighteen inches above the surface so that the loons had merely to dive off into the water (or out of the water on to the nest), and this was of the greatest importance since evolution has designed these birds for floating and diving rather than for progress on dry land. They could not, in fact, walk as other birds do because their legs were too near their tails with all the weight in front, so on land they had to slide along on their breasts using their short legs to propel themselves as they did in the water.

The muskrats are peaceful folk with much of the cleverness and engineering skill of the beavers. Being vegetarians they are good neighbours, though certainly they can fight when they need to. By the time the mother loon was ready to take her seat on the roof, there were already five blind and hairless atoms of muskrathood squirming about in the nursery just below and she must plainly have heard their whimperings. Unlike the rats the big loons were not popular among the other water fowl, for they are jealous of their territory and do not want competition. So the grebes and the ducks and the coots and the waterhens steered clear of Thunder Bay as soon as they saw the big loon sitting on the muskrat house, for they were afraid of her deadly bayonet bill. Also they disliked the loons' methods of attack, for when they saw a trespasser innocently sailing in their bay they would come up from below and prod the unsuspecting bird in the stomach with their beaks. When the trespasser was gone—and that did not usually take long—the loons would rise to the surface and, standing up in the water, would utter their ringing and triumphant cries which set a thousand echoes going. Then they would cruise around with eyes shining savagely and feathers on end, and an angry loon low in the water can look very dangerous indeed.

The result was that all that summer they had Thunder Bay to themselves, but there were plenty of similar bays all round the long narrow sheet of water and plenty of room for everyone. As for diving, the loons were certainly the super-experts of all normally inland birds for they have even been found in the sea nets at the terrific pressures of 300 feet, so they would easily have searched the bottom of any part of their beaver-created home lake.

The aggression of the two loons was to prove a blessing to their nearest neighbours, the muskrats, and even before the first egg was laid an opportunity occurred of their paying off their rent liberally. Luckily the parent muskrats were at home when the mink, which haunted the swamp nearby, found and raided their dwelling. The male rat must have met him in deep water at the entrance of the passageway and, fighting for life, he prevented him from forcing an entrance till both of them rose panting for air, the mink to the surface alongside the house, the muskrat to their drying-chamber, while his wife stood by ready for her turn. But it seemed, alas, that they were as good as doomed, and that the mink would return time after time till he finally succeeded in beating them and destroying their family.

But as things panned out he did not return at all for the female loon also was at home. She saw the wicked, wedge-shaped head break surface almost alongside her, and quick as lightning she struck. That bayonet bill aimed at the eye and she struck to kill, only just missing her mark, but she gashed one side of the killer's face from eye to nose, and he dived with a savage chuckle and made

134

off under water. Never again did he go anywhere near the muskrat house.

Soon after this episode two olive-brown eggs were laid, rather bilious-looking affairs flaked with muddy red, and during the days that followed the parent loons trod on them, sat on them, and turned them till they became muddier and muddier. We may wonder how birds manage to love their eggs as they do, for nothing could be less responsive than an egg; yet to the two loons they were the most precious things in all their world of woods and waters and weed, and they would have fought to the death in defence of them. Always one of them was in attendance on the nest, and though the other might be sailing a mile away they kept in touch by their calling. How one comes to love those wild sad cries and peal after peal of crazy laughter echoing miles through the woods, now near, now far! It broke the great silence of the lake day and night till it became a part of the wide waters and the still forests. The lake itself was always changing: one minute it was like a great mirror reflecting the blue skies and stooping trees, the next ruffled by cat's-paws of wind or leaden under the clouds of thunder. At sunset it became a vast sea of colour and the boy who lived in the long cabin by the boathouse would stand on the landing-stage with his hands behind him, thinking his own long thoughts.

Sometimes the loons' wild notes would stir the coyotes into their evening song, and the many echoes would disturb the waders from the gravel beds and their thin piping notes would be added to the chorus. Then the silence of the great woods would fall like the closing of a door, and as the sun dipped from view behind the tree tops, the chill of night would creep in—for at that altitude the nights were always cold.

Every lake and every bay had its own individuality, its own lights and shadows and personal atmosphere of friendliness, and the sounds of spring in the mountains. There were many such bays as Thunder Bay on those many miles of waterfront, and the anglers knew each by some feature of its own, some interest with which nature had endowed it and made it dear to their hearts. There was the bay with the eagles' eyrie in a tall Douglas, the bay of the fish-hawks, and Flameflower Bay with its soft display of crimson. Thunder Bay always had something to offer, for near to the muskrat house was the drinking-place where many of the big folk came to refresh themselves. There, if anywhere, you would see the panther pausing at the water's edge. How long and silken and graceful she was with her peaceful, almost melancholy face, and seeing her thus one would never have thought that she was the biggest murderer of deer in all the woods. She would pause with head aside, admiring her own reflection like a vain and beautiful lady at her mirror, even patting at it with a graceful forepaw till it became distorted into ripples. The wolf and the coyote also came to drink and when one of these big hunters appeared, the loon on her nest near by would sink slowly into the dome until she was a part of it. It was quite different however when the mule deer or even the giant moose came down, for then the loon would look at the visitor bright-eyed and chunter a few notes of greeting. Once, when the hen bird was sitting, the mink came and glared at her through the rushes as though to let her see his scarred face, and the loon hissed at him with neck feathers ruffled and beak half open. He went away without a sound, but left an evil atmosphere behind him as though he had told her that some day he would get even with her. But when he was gone she hooted and cackled her mockery and derision.

For all their territorial jealousy the loons did not like to see their neighbours in misfortune and there was an affair in the tree tops that caused no end of a stir. Not a quarter of a mile away, on one of the headlands, the Blue Herons had built their huge nest of sticks in the top of a tall cedar and it already contained fledglings whose heads could occasionally be seen wobbling above the eyrie. One hot afternoon when dragonflies of many colours hovered and darted among the rushes, the loon on the nest saw a long dark outline rapidly climbing up through the branches towards the herons' nest. She stood up immediately and started to make the woods and the waters ring with her wild alarm. The parent herons were not at home, but their nest was obviously the object of the agile climber, and he was already within twelve feet of it. The other loon rose into the air half a mile away and, echoing the cries of its mate, flew with rapidly beating wings towards the scene of threatened tragedy. Round and round the big nest it flew crying desperately, and doubtless it was this warning which brought one of the herons headlong from the skies to defend its young.

Alighting on the edge of the nest the old bird's method of defence was safe, simple and easy. Not a feather was ruffled, for it simply emptied the contents of its crop—essence of fish, and that particularly evil and tenacious glue the blue heron has the power of secreting in just such emergencies—all over the raider. The king of the martens (for it was he) simply let go his hold and fell a sheer thirty feet, then hastily scrambled down from branch to branch, while the voices of the loons sank into one long-drawn and melancholy note of approval.

A few days later the two loon eggs hatched out and the down-covered chicks took to the water almost immediately with their parents. Until darkness fell all four cruised silently about Thunder Bay, the parents on either side and not till night came did they proceed proudly to tell the world that the great event had occurred. For once their strong voices were entirely joyous, long peals of cackling laughter, tailing off into bugle notes and bubblings, and presently the man who looked after the boats and served the fishermen, said to his son that something must have disturbed the loons. The boy thought maybe it was a bear swimming about in the lake after the day's heat and with the notes still ringing this led to a general discussion concerning loons, for the boy was immensely interested in them.

"My little bird book says that they live entirely on fish," he announced. "They can swallow only small ones because there is a kind of a size gauge in their throats, but I calculate they must eat water weeds too."

His father replied that the man who wrote the book *should* know something about it since it had cost several dollars. "All the same," he added, "when I was a boy, I lived by a little prairie lake which was too alkaline for fish to live in, but every year a pair of loons brought up their chicks."

"Perhaps they fed on dragonflies," the boy suggested, but his father answered: "There weren't any dragonflies either. In their larva stage they live in the water like the fish, so they could no more live than the fish could."

Now the boy, being a born naturalist, realized that the first thing to learn about any wild creature is its foods, so the following Saturday he took his canoe and his fishing rod and paddled up the lake. He found the loon family in Thunder Bay, and immediately he was round the headland the old loons stood up in the water lashing their wings and came dashing across the surface in a display of defence, but the chicks were unafraid of him. He got quite close to them and he would dearly have loved to take one in his hands and examine it, but instead he began to toss towards them the food he had brought—bits of dry biscuits and bread, the remains of a can of green peas and even one or two sardines from the bottom of a tin. The wild birds of the lake were frequently fed from the luncheon canisters of fishermen. So that very soon he had a flotilla of coots, waterhens, and gorgeously coloured wood ducks eagerly seizing the morsels, but neither old loons nor young would touch a fragment of the food he offered. He was, however, to learn that loons sometimes eat flies, for his fly rod was over the end of the boat with line and cast trailing in the water, and when he took up his paddle the line suddenly tightened and the end of the rod began to bob. He thought he had hooked a good fish, but on reeling in he found to his dismay that it was one of the young loons which had taken the fly and firmly hooked itself.

Then followed some breathless seconds, for as he drew the chick closer and closer to the boat the old birds went mad with anxiety and fury, and as he put out the landing net and drew the youngster aboard he really thought they were going to climb in after it. They struck against the freeboard with their dangerous beaks, and truly he had never seen wild birds so angry. At the same time he was having trouble with the chick, which also had a formidable beak. It bit and stabbed at his hands till the blood streamed and eventually he had to tie its beak with a loop of string, after which the small hook was easily disengaged from the corner of its beak. So he was thankful to restore it to the water and its anxious parents, and it was thus that he learnt a naturalist's first great lesson, namely, that the kindest and wisest way to treat a wild creature is to leave it strictly alone.

Before the chicks were three-quarters grown, and they grew very rapidly, there was another example of how well their parents were able to look after them. These were slack days at the lakeside when few anglers arrived to fish from the boats, and the boy's father spent many a half-hour watching the water birds and tying flies. Most often he watched the ospreys fishing and he had come to love them best since they seemed at peace with the other birds, even with the eagles which so persistently robbed them of their catches. Though hawks, they seemed to bear no malice towards anyone, but went industriously on with their own job of carrying fish for their young, and what he saw that day did not endear the loons to him any further.

He was watching an osprey circling high up and quite close in looking for fish, and saw it dive and strike the water with a splash almost alongside the loons. The two young ones dashed across the surface, peeping their terror, and before the osprey could lift its catch one of the old loons struck at it and brought it down. The osprey lay on the surface, its beautiful wings outspread and as it floated it raised its crested head and uttered a plaintive cry to its mate, still free in the heavens. The fishing guide feared it was mortally wounded, and taking a boat he rowed out and took it in his hands. A crimson patch was spreading over its mottled breast, and when he got back to the landing-stage the boy was waiting for him.

"Them varmints the loons!" the man muttered as he handed the injured bird to his son. "For two straws I'd take the gun to the spiteful creatures!"

The boy did not want that to happen, and he took the osprey gently in his hands and carried it home. He dressed the wound and for many days tended it, catching fish to supply the bird's needs, and keeping it in the half-light so that it would not struggle. Before very long it seemed recovered and he let it go at their door. At once it flew off to its eyrie on the pine ridge, and he saw the pair circling over their young, their thin-edge cries of joy floating down like silver flakes of confetti. It was one of those rare occasions when man can be of great help to the wild folk, and the boy slept the happier that night.

By mid-July the parent loons took to cruising apart, each with a chick. This was apparently to distribute the fishing, and the young birds looked now as big as their parents as they floated low in the water. The chicks were a dull brown in contrast with the dark plumage of the adults and they were without the white necklaces and the white pearls on their backs, visible from afar when they were swimming.

One day when the fishing guide and his son sat by the boathouse with nothing much to talk about, the man nodded towards two of the birds fishing near and

140

remarked: "I bet you don't know how the loon got its white necklace!"

Admittedly the boy did not know, so his father told him the story:

"It was long ago, before the lake was given its long Indian name, almost forgotten now because Loon Lake is shorter. The Indian village stood where the Fishing Lodge stands now, and the Indians of these mountains lived in what amounted to holes in the ground, deep enough to keep out the wind. The fire stood in the centre and the hole was roofed over with branches.

"One year winter came early and was terrible in its severity so that the caribou took a different route and never came near the lake. The result was that by Christmas the Indians were starving, and the hungry wolves took to killing the dogs till the tribesmen were afraid that they would be taking the children next. The packs were led by a big black wolf, such as we sometimes get today migrating down from Alaska.

"Anyway the Indians were destitute and starving, and their Chief was so old that he was almost blind and could no longer lead his hunters. So the old warrior, who had been a great man, went out into the woods to consult his gods, and when he returned he told his people that he was to make a great journey alone—away to the mighty Sarrinach River which is too turbulent to freeze and where the loons spend the winter. The loon was the emblem of the tribe, carved in grotesque representations on their totem poles, and only the loons could advise them in their dreadful dilemma.

"In vain the people of the village argued and entreated, pointing out that the Chief was too old to make such a journey in dead of winter. The old man set out and somehow he made his way over the mountains until he found the chief of the loons fishing on the deep water below the falls. When he had explained his mission the loon dived to a great depth in order to consult its gods, staying so long under the water that the old man feared it had drowned. At length it bobbed up and told him that his hunters must first kill the black wolf and then their troubles would come to an end.

"According to Indian custom, civility demanded a gift to the bird for its services, but the old Chief had nothing to give but the necklace of fossilized shells round his neck. So, unfastening it, he tossed it out to the loon and it fell about the bird's neck. It entwined itself where the bird now wears its white necklace, but in falling it broke and some of the shells showered across the bird's back—hence the loons' shell necklace and the flakes like pearls upon its back."

"Yes," agreed the boy gravely, "that was all right, but how did the old Chief reach home?"

"Walked!" replied his father. "Somehow he managed to grope his way back over the mountain tops, and his people were overjoyed to see him alive. The hunters organized a great batteau and killed the black wolf, whereupon the rest of the pack fled howling into the forest; the storms ceased, and the period of famine was at an end. When the old man died they gave the lake his name, but as I have said it is almost forgotten, and even the Indians call it 'Loon Lake'."

The wonderful summer drew to a close, and after that came the Indian Summer with its slanting sunbeams and drifting of crimson and golden leaves. The thin ice began to creep out from the lake margins, the blackbirds and humming-birds departed and one thing worried the boy—that he had not yet seen the young loons take to the air. Soon they would have to make the grim journey over the mountains to the Sarrinach River or perhaps farther still, following the swallows to the Gulf States.

Frequently of late he had seen the old birds stand up in the water flapping their wings while the two chicks obediently followed their exercise, but when a parent bird dashed across the surface till it was airborne, or flew over them calling and bidding them rise, the chicks would shake their heads indifferently and go on with their fishing. How were they to reach the waters which never freeze if they had not learnt to fly?

The boy and his father stood by the boathouse one cold dark evening. The frost was keen though there was no light in the sky and now and then the booming of the ice thundered across the stillness. The ice was closing and that day the ospreys and the eagles had gone. Were they all to go? The squirrels still chattered in the branches and the little striped chipmunks were still garnering their harvests. The ice had closed on all sides, and there remained only one great sheet of open water far out in the centre of the lake, and there the four loons were assembled, the last now to leave.

The two old loons seemed desperate. Night was not far off, and time and again they rose into the air, leaving long white wakes behind them, bidding their young to rise. But the chicks still seemed reluctant, till at last one of them spread its long, tapered wings and emulating its parent skimmed from the surface. Higher and higher it rose, calling triumphantly, appearing as strong and able as the old birds; then the other chick followed, so that all four were flying. Still higher they rose, and so great was their speed that they had soon encircled the lake, looking down upon all the scenes of the summer, the lagoons of the musquash swamp where small fish swarmed, the beaver ponds at the outlet, the tall trees at Thunder Point and the old Indian fish trap by the meadow. They rose steadily until they were the merest specks in the heavens and they turned their beaks southwards. And so, farewell!

Yes, farewell! The loons vanished against the white barrier of the mountains, and silence finally fell upon the cold world. It was the beginning of the long silence of winter, no sound now for eight white months save occasionally the harsh scream of lynx or panther, the croaking of the ravens or the melancholy rally call of the timber wolves. The boy slipped his arm into his father's .

"Dad," he said, "the loons of summer are gone," and as he spoke the first feathery flakes of snow began to fall.

Destiny

FRANK PENN-SMITH

"You splashed me!" shrieked the Hen.

"Get away, you fussy thing!" barked the Pig, with both feet in the trough.

"Faugh!" cried the Hen, "none but the dirtiest chicks stand in the dish! You've more there than you can eat," she continued.

The Pig looked at her with twinkling eyes: he considered for a moment. He was deep, that Pig. "Well, well!" he grumbled. "Eat your fill, but don't go picking the peas out." And he was soon guzzling again, chin-deep, keeping his keen eyes upon her; while she, with one frightened eye upon him, choked over the lumpy food.

Her crop was full: tuck it away as she would from under her chin, it rolled back there like a balloon. She suddenly left off eating and swiftly stropped her bill on the trough edge.

"Now I'll go and peep in there!" she said to herself, marching off towards the Pig's sleeping apartment.

It was very damp, and she stepped daintily; standing on a stone, she peered into the darkness.

"Come out of that!" roared the Pig. "If you lay there I'll eat the eggs!"

"Don't trouble yourself," cried the Hen, "I don't like rooms on the ground floor, especially when they are under water." The Pig answered nothing: she had the last word, but he had his way.

Next morning she was, as usual, first in the food-rush,

145

and pecked fifteen to the Brahma's ten, but when the rest of the hens were chasing after the Frizzled Fowl with an apple in her beak she slipped off by herself. On the way to the pigsty she had a great fright, and arrived cackling nervously.

"What's the matter now?" said the Pig.

"There's a man at the back door," she cackled, "with feathers on his chin and a great white comb."

The Pig considered for a moment. "That's the man who buys the calves," he said. "I always like him to come, because there's always lots of sour milk afterwards. That's a beard on his chin," he went on, "and it isn't feathers, it's bristles."

From that moment they were friends, and he let her eat what she liked.

The Pig was treated like a prince, and fed on the fat of the land, but they never let him out of the sty. He had something on his mind. Anyone who knew him could see it.

One day the Hen said to him: "Sheep are good meat—underneath the wool."

"Of course!" he replied, "but how do you know?"

"They are skinning one out yonder," she said, "and I got some pickings."

He looked strangely at her. "What they do to *one*, they might do to *another*," he said darkly.

He had a plan.

He made her bring him all the news. He gave her good advice. "Never try to do two things at once," he would say. Moreover, he said, "Never attempt to *sit* without telling me."

She did not understand, but she promised. Now he had a profound knowledge of the farmyard, and could even remember when they milked into a kerosene tin.

"Your mother," he said to her one day, "was the Incubator. I remember when you were hatched, and a fine fuss they made. The Incubator," he went on, "eats no food; they only give it hot water."

One day the Hen never appeared.

What had happened?

This had happened.

She was *sitting*.

It had come suddenly upon her. She became, as it were, clouded over and she clucked. A desire seized her to tuck in everything around.

She rolled the pot egg from the next nest into her own.

Then she worked up her eyes, as you do when you drink.

Then she forgot everything, and she no longer knew yesterday from tomorrow.

Weeks after she awoke, hearing squeaks from the nest beneath her. "Hush!" she cried, "you will wake the eggs," for she still wandered a little.

But it was the chicks coming out. She could not tell where they came from. She pushed them back when they put their heads out.

When she considered it again, perhaps these *were* the chicks she was to hatch. Only half had come out—the rest were still eggs.

What was to be done? Should she take the chicks and risk the eggs? Or should she hatch the eggs and risk the chicks?

She would consult the Pig.

The Pig!

He would be *furious*.

She had been *sitting*.

She got up hastily and rushed towards the pigsty, her chicks with her. She was very giddy. Half-way there she encamped. The eggs went cold.

She rushed back to the fowlhouse: the Black Hen with her chicks stood in the doorway. The chickens mingled. Which were which? They were all alike.

By this time she was frantic: who would save her eggs?

She rushed back to the nest, and the Black Hen marched off triumphantly with all the chicks.

She turned the eggs over with her beak: they were cold, addled.

With only half her feathers she came back to the pigsty.

He looked at her out of the corner of his eye. He was fatter than ever, and twice as solemn.

"Where have you been all this time?" he asked huskily.

"Why?" she asked nervously.

"I should have found out something," he said gloomily, "but your everlasting sitting has done it. Too late! Too late!" he said.

She gaped at him —her beak open, her legs apart.

Suddenly he turned upon her: "Where do the Pigs go that disappear?" he asked hoarsely.

She sank to the ground. She got up. She ran to the fowlhouse and hid behind a bin. When the hens came in to roost she hid herself between the fattest of them.

Daybreak came at last: it was very cold.

"Get up!" said the Brown Hen, nudging the White.

"Get up yourself!" growled the other.

The Frizzled Fowl unwreathed its neck. "It's the moon," she said, and curled up again on the perch.

She said that because she wished it so. The Pig's Hen awoke in agony. She dropped down stealthily, she fell on the Black Hen and chicks, she squealed and gurgled. She rushed over them and darted to the sty.

The Pig came out before his empty trough, smelling at the dark dawn. She dashed into the sty, and, slipping on the frosty floor, fell. The Pig laughed: then he smelt the air again.

"I wish I belonged to the Man in Spectacles," he said dreamily.

"Why?" inquired the Hen in an early morning tone of voice.

"Because he is a Vegetarian," said the Pig.

"What does that mean?" quavered the Hen.

"He doesn't eat Pork," said the Pig.

"Does he eat—Fowl?" she asked, hesitating cautiously.

"Perhaps not," said the Pig.

She was beginning to cackle with fright, but she gulped it down. "Let us fly!" she gasped.

"*I* don't fly," he said solemnly, "and one of your wings is clipped." This was true.

She began running in the dawning light. She stopped at intervals and peered round. Somehow she found herself on the fence. She lurched backwards and forwards, divided in mind whether to go into hysterics or to run away to the Man in Spectacles.

If she fell off on *this* side she would go into hysterics. If she fell off on *that* she would run away to the Man in Spectacles. She fell off on that side.

That day the Man in Spectacles had a fowl too many, but as he was very short-sighted he could not tell which.

So he said nothing.

But the Pigeons, passing over the pigsty, saw that it was empty.

The Heller

HENRY WILLIAMSON

In March the high spring-tides lap with their ragged and undulating riband of flotsam the grasses near the top of the sea-wall; and once in a score of years the south-west gale piles the sea in the estuary so high that it lops over the bank and rushes down to the reclaimed grazing marsh within. The land-locked water returns on the ebb by way of the reedy dykes, through the culverts under the wall with their one-way hinged wooden doors, and by muddy channels to the sea again.

I was unfortunate enough to miss seeing such a flood following the Great Gale, when many big trees, most of them elms but not a few beech and oak, went down; but hearing of it, I went down to the marsh the next afternoon before the time of high tide, hoping to see the water brimming over again. I wandered along the sea-wall, where the hoof-holed path of clay still held sea-water, as far as the black hospital ship *Nyphen*, and then I returned. The gale had blown itself out, a blue sky lay beyond Hartland Point, far out over the calm Atlantic.

There is a slanting path leading to the road below by the marshman's cottage, and by this I left the wide prospect seen from the sea-wall. While descending I noticed that the grasses down the inner slope were washed flat and straggly by the heavy overflooding of the day before.

The marshman was standing in the porch of the cottage, looking at his ducklings which had hatched about a fortnight since. He wore his spectacles and had a book in his hands. We greeted each other, and I stopped to talk.

I always enjoyed talking with the marshman. His face pleased me. I liked his kind brown eyes, his grey hair, his small and intelligent sea-brown face. His dog had recently been kicked by a bullock, and had a broken leg which the marshman had set with a wooden splint. This knocked on the ground as the dog trotted about with apparent ease. The marshman was a skilful man: I remembered how he had saved the life of a sheep the year before, when it was staggering crazily, because, said the marshman, it had a worm in its brain. The marshman had held the sheep's head between his knees, cut a hole in its skull with a knife, and drawn out the tape-worm by suction through a quill cut from the pinion feather of a goose. It was an even chance, for most sheep so afflicted have to be destroyed. This ewe got well, and—but the story is about the mysterious loss of the marshman's ducklings, not of mutton.

In a soft voice he began telling me about the book in his hands, which he said was "wonderful and most interesting". It was thick, and heavy, and printed in small, close-set type. It was *The History of the Jews,* and the marshman had been reading it with the same care and patience with which, year after year, he had cut the reeds in the dykes, and scythed the thistles in the rank grass. For years he had been reading that book, and he had not yet reached the middle pages.

Would I like to take the book home with me and have a read of it? He was a bit busy just now and could easily spare it for a day or two. I was quite welcome to take it, if . . .

I was saved from a reply by the sudden change in the marshman's face. He was staring intently beyond the gate by which we stood. His spectacles were pushed back from his eyes. I looked in the direction of his stare, and saw the usual scene—fowls on the stony and feathery road, and a couple of pigs nosing among them; the down-hanging branches of the willow tree over the dyke; the green pointed leaves of the flag-iris rising thickly along both banks; the sky-gleams between them. On the water a brood of yellowish-white ducklings were paddling, watched anxiously from the road by the hen that had hatched them.

"The heller!"

At the muttered angry words the marshman's dog, which had assumed a stiff attitude from the moment of his master's fixed interest in something as yet unsmelled, unseen, and unheard by itself, whined and crouched and sprang over the gate. It had gone a few yards, sending the hens clucking and flying in all directions, when the marshman shouted. Seeing its master's arm flung to the left, the dog promptly turned in that direction. I saw its hackles rise. The narrow dyke, which brought fresh drinking water to the grazing marsh, was crossed under the willow tree by a clammer or single heavy plank of elm-wood. As the dog ran on to the clammer I saw something at the farther end slide into the water. I had a fleeting impression of the vanishing hindquarters of a squat and slender dog, dark brown as a bulrush, and with the palms of its feet widely webbed as a duck's. It had a long tail, tapering to a point. The brown tail slid over the plank flatly yet swiftly, and disappeared without splash into the slight ripple made by the submerging animal.

" 'Tis that darned old mousey-coloured fitch," grumbled the marshman opening the gate. "It be after my ducklings. It took one just about this time yesterday. Yurr, Ship!" to the dog. "Fetch un, Ship!" The dog sprang around barking raucously, and trotted along the plank again, nose between paws, and whining with excitement where the otter had stood. Then it looked at its master and barked at the water.

While it was barking the ducklings, about fifteen yards away, began to run on the water, beating their little flukey stumps of wings and stretching out their necks. *Queep! Queep! Queep!* they cried. The foster-hen on the bank was clucking and jerking her comb about in agitation.

"Ah, you heller, you!" cried the marshman, as a duckling was drawn under by invisible jaws. The other ducklings waddled out by the brimming edge of the road, made for the hen in two files of uniform and tiny yellowish bodies aslant with straining to reach the cover of wings. Very red and jerky about the comb and cheek-pendules, with flickering eyes, this motherly fowl squatted on the stones and lowered her wings till they rested on her useless pinion shafts, and fluffed out her feathers to make room for the eight mites which, in spite of her constant calls and entreaties, would persist in walking on that cold and unwalkable place, which was only for sipping-from at the edge.

Peep peep peep, quip pip queep weep, whistled the ducklings drowsily, in their sweet and feeble voices.

The marshman came out of the cottage with a gun.

"The heller!" he said. "The withering beast, it ought to be kicked to flames."

He waited five minutes, watching the water where the duckling had gone down.

Parallel lines of ripples, wavering with infirm and milk-white sky, rode along the brimming water. The tide was still rising. Twenty yards away the young strong leaves of the flag-irises began to quiver. We waited. The *peep-peeps* of the happy ducklings ceased.

Water began to run, in sudden starts, around the smoothed stones in the roadway. The tide was rising fast. A feather was carried twirling on a runnel that stopped by my left toe; and after a pause it ran on a few inches, leaving dry specks of dust and bud-sheaths tacked to the welt.

The outline of the dyke was lost in the overbrimming of the water. Grasses began to float and stray at its edges. The runnels curiously explored the least hollow; running

153

forward, pausing, turning sideways or backwards, and blending, as though gladly, with one another.

"It be gone," said the marshman, lowering the gun, to my relief, for its double barrels had been near my cheek, and they were rusty, thin as an egg-shell at the muzzle, and loaded with an assortment of broken screw-heads, nuts, and odd bits of iron. He was as economical with his shooting as he was with his reading. Originally the gun had been a flintlock, owned by his great-grandfather; and his father had had it converted into a percussion cap. Its walnut stock was riddled with worm-holes; and even as I was examining it, I heard the sound like the ticking of a watch, which ceased after nine ticks. The death-watch beetle. It was doubtful which would go first—the stock "falling abroad" in its tunnelled brittleness, or the barrels bursting from frail old-age.

"It's a high spring tide," I said, stepping farther back. "I suppose the otter came up on it, and down the dyke?"

Then the marshman told me about the "heller". We stood with our backs to the deep and ancient thorn hedge that borders the road to the east, a hedge double-sheared by wind and man, six feet high and eight feet thick and so matted that a man could walk along it without his boots sinking. It was grey and gold with lichens. I had always admired the hedge by the marsh toll-gate. I leaned gingerly against it while the marshman told me that he had seen the otter on the two afternoons previously, and both times when the tide was nearly on the top of the flood. No, it did not come up the dyke; it was a bold beast, and came over the sea-wall, where the tide had poured over two afternoons ago. "My wife zeed'n running over the wall, like a little brown dog. I reckon myself th' heller comes from the duckponds over in Heanton marsh, and sleeps by day in th' daggers. Otters be always travellin' up the pill vor to get to the duckponds or goin' on up to the pillhead, and over the basin of the weir into fresh water, after trout. Never before have I heard tell of an otter going time after time, and by day, too, after the same ducklings."

I was listening intently. Was that a low, flute-like whistle . . . ?

"Tis most unusual, zur, for an artter will always take fish when he can get fish, eels particularly, and there be plenty of eels all over the marsh. An arrter loveth an eel; 'tis its most natural food, in a manner of speaking. 'Tis what is called an ambulance baste, the arrter be, yes 'tis like a crab, that can live in both land and water, a proper ambulance baste it be. A most interestin' baste, for those that possess th' education vor to study up all that sort of thing. Now can 'ee tell me how an artter serves an eel different from another fish? Other fish, leastways those I've zin with my own eyes, are ate head downwards; but an eel be ate tail virst, and the head and shoulders be left. I've a' zin scores of eels, and all ate tail virst!"

While the old fellow was speaking, the water in irregular pourings and innocent swirls was stealing right across the road. It reached the hen, who, to judge from the downward pose of her head, regarded it as a nuisance. A runnel slipped stealthily between her cane-coloured feet, wetting the claws worn with faithful scratching for the young. She arose, and strutted away in the lee of the hedge, calling her brood; and *Wock! Wock! Wet!* she cried, for with tiny notes of glee the ducklings had headed straight for the wide water gleaming with the early sunset.

The marshman said, "Darn the flood!" for *The History of the Jews*, container of future years' laborious pleasure, lay in a plash by the gate ten strides away. He picked it up, regarding ruefully the dripping cover. He was saying that it wasn't no odds, a bit of damp on the outside, when I noticed a small travelling ripple in the shape of an arrow moving out from the plank now almost awash. It continued steadily for about three yards from the plank, and then the arrow-head ceased to push. Ripples spread out slowly, and beyond the ripples a line of bubbles like shot

155

began to rise and lie still. The line, increasing steadily by lengths varying from two or three to a dozen inches, drew out towards the ducklings.

I took long strides forward beside the marshman. Our footfalls splashed in the shallow water. The dog trotted at his heels, quivering, its ears cocked. A swirl arose in the leat and rocked the ducklings; they cried and struck out for the grass, but one stayed still, trying to rise on weeny wings, and then it went under.

"The *heller!*" cried the marshman, raising his gun.

For about twenty seconds we waited.

A brown whiskered head, flat and seal-like, with short rough hairs and beady black eyes, looked out of the water. *Bang!* It dived at the flash, and although we peered and waited for at least a minute after the whining of a screw-head ricocheting away over the marsh had ceased, I saw only our spectral faces shaking the water.

The next afternoon I went down by the eastern sea-wall, and lay on the flat grassy ridge, with a view of the lower end of the Ram's-horn duckpond. Wildfowl were flying round the marsh and settling on the open water hidden between thick green reeds. Many scores had their nests in the preserve. Why did the otter, I wondered, come all the way to the dyke when it could take all the ducklings it wanted in the pond? Perhaps in my reasoning I was falling into the old error of ascribing to a wild beast something of human reasoning; for had I been an otter after ducklings I should certainly have stayed where they were most numerous.

The tide flowed past me, with its usual straggle of froth covering the flotsam of corks, bottles, clinker, spruce-bark from the Bideford shipyards, tins, cabbage leaves and sticks. Two ketches rode up on the flood, the exhausts of their oil engines echoing with hollow thuds over mud and water. I wondered why they were wasting oil, when the current was so swift to carry them; but when they made fast to their mooring-buoys, and the bows swung round, I realized the use of the engines—to keep them head-on in the fairway. Of course! Gulls screamed as they floated around the masts and cordage of the black craft, awaiting the dumping overboard of garbage. I waited for an hour, but saw nothing of the otter.

"Did ee see'n?" asked the marshman when I went back. His gun lay on the table, and Ship the dog was crouched on the threshold, nose on paws pointing to the clammer bridge over the dyke.

"He's took another duckling," growled the man.

The otter must have made an early crossing while I was lazing on the bank. Perhaps he had come through a culvert, squeezing past the sodden wooden trap; and then, either seeing or winding me, had crossed under water. The marshman, happening to come to the door, had seen the duckling going under, and although he had waited for ten minutes, nothing had come up.

"Ship here went nosing among the daggers, but couldn't even get wind of 'n. I reckon that ambulance baste can lie on the bottom and go to sleep if it has a mind to."

By ambulance he meant amphibious, I imagined. An otter has no gills; it breathes in the ordinary way, being an animal that has learned to swim and hunt under water.

"Didn't you see even a bubble?"

"Not one!"

It seemed strange. Also, it had seemed strange that the engines of the ketches were "wasting" oil. That had a perfectly ordinary explanation . . . when one realized it!

"And it took a duck in just the same way as before?"

"That's it! In a wink, that duck went down under."

"But didn't the ducklings see the otter?"

"Noomye! The poor li'l butie was took quick as a wink." He was much upset by it.

"Now I'll tell ee what I'll do," he said. "I'll till a gin for a rat, I will, and if I trap an artter, well, 'twill be a pity, as the artter-'untin' gentry would say; but there 'tis!"

Otters were not generally trapped in the country of the

Taw and Torridge rivers, as most of the riparian-owners subscribed to the otter-hounds. There were occasions, however, when a gin was tilled, or set, on a submerged rock where an otter was known to touch, or on a sunken post driven into the river-bed near its holt. About once in a season the pack drew the brackish waters of the Ram's-horn Duckpond, but an otter was very rarely killed there, as there was impregnable holding among the thick reeds. I looked at the marshman's face, filled with grim thoughts about the heller (had he got the term from *The History of the Jews*?) and remembered how, only the year before, when an otter had been killed near Branton Church, he had confided to me that he didn't care much for "artter-'untin' "; that it was "not much sport with all they girt dogs agin one small baste".

"I've got some old rabbit gins," said the marshman. "And I'll till them on the clammer, and get that heller, I will."

I went away to watch the mating flight of the golden plover over the marsh, and the sun had gone down behind the low line of the sandhills to the west, when I returned along the sea-wall. Three rabbit gins—rusty affairs of open iron teeth and flat steel springs ready to snap and hold anything that trod on them—lay on the plank. The marshman had bound lengths of twisted brass rabbit-wire around the plank and through the ends of the chains, so that, dragged into the dyke, the weight of the three gins would drown any struggling otter.

My road home lay along the edge of the dyke, which was immediately under the sea-wall. Old upturned boats, rusty anchors, rotting bollards of tree-trunks and other gear lay on the wall and its inner grassy slope. Near the pill-head the brown ribs of a ketch, almost broken up, lay above the wall. I came to the hump where the road goes over the culvert. Leaning on the stone parapet, I watched the fresh water of the river moving with dark eddies under the fender into the dyke, and the overflow tumbling into the concrete basin of the weir and sliding down the short length to the rising tide. It barely rippled. The air was still and clear, bright with eve-star and crescent moon.

The last cart had left the Great Field, the faint cries of lambs arose under the moon, men were all home to their cottages, or playing skittles in the village inns. Resting the weight of my body on the stone, I stared vaguely at the water, thinking how many strange impulses and feelings came helter-skelter out of a man, and how easy it was to judge him falsely by any one act or word. The marshman had pitied a hunted otter; he had raged against a hunting otter; he felt tenderly and protectively towards the ducklings; he would complacently stab their necks when the peas ripened, and sell them for as much money as he could get for them. In the future he would not think otter-hunting a cruel sport. And if the otter-hunters heard that he had trapped and drowned an otter, they would be sincerely upset that it had suffered such a cruel and, as it were, an unfair death. Perhaps the only difference between animal and man was that the animal had fewer notions ...

I was musing in this idle manner, my thoughts slipping away as water, when I heard a sound somewhere behind me. It was a thin piercing whistle, the cry of an otter. Slowly I moved back my head, till only a part of my face would be visible in silhouette from the water below. I watched for a bubble, a sinuous shadow, an arrowy ripple, a swirl; I certainly did not expect to see a fat old dog-otter come drifting down on his back, swishing with his rudder and bringing it down with great thwacking splashes on the water while he chewed a half-pound trout held in his short paws. My breath ceased; my eyes held from blinking. I had a perfect view of his sturdy body, the yellowish-white patch of fur on his belly below his ribs, his sweeping whiskers, his dark eyes. Still chewing, he bumped head-on into the sill, kicked himself upright, walked on the concrete, and stood there crunching, while the five pools running from his legs and rudder ran into one. He did not chew, as I had read in books of otters chewing; he just stood there on his four legs, the tail-half of the trout sticking out of his mouth, and gulped down the bits. That trout disappeared in about ten seconds. Then the otter leaned down to the water and lapped as a cat does.

He was old, slow, coarse-haired, and about thirty pounds in weight—the biggest otter I had seen, with the broadest head.

After quenching his thirst he put his head and shoulders under water, holding himself from falling in by his stumpy webbed forefeet, and his rudder, eighteen inches long, pressing down straight behind. He was watching the fish. As though any fish remained in the water-flow after that dreaded apparition had come splashing under the culvert!

With the least ripple he slid into the water. I breathed and blinked with relief, but dared not move otherwise. A head looked up almost immediately, and two dark eyes stared at me. The otter sneezed, shook the water out of his small ears, and sank away under. I expected it to be my last sight of the beast, and leaning over to see if an arrowy ripple pointed upstream I knocked a piece of loose stone off the parapet. To my amazement he came up near the sill again, with something in his mouth. He swung over on his back, and bit it in play. He climbed on to the sill and dropped it there, and slipped back into the water. It was the stone that had dropped from the parapet!

I kept still. The otter reappeared with something white in his mouth. He dropped it with a tinkle beside the stone, and the tinkle must have pleased him, for he picked up the china sherd—it looked like part of a teacup with the handle—and rolled over with it in his paws.

As in other Devon waters, the stream was a pitching place for cottage rubbish; and during the time I was standing by the parapet watching the otter at his play he had collected about a dozen objects—rusty salmon tins, bits of broken glass, sherds of clome pitchers and jamjars, and one-half of a sheep's jaw. He ranged them on the sill of the weir, tapping the more musical with a paw, as a cat does, until they fell into the water, when he would dive for and retrieve them.

At the end of about half an hour the sea was lapping over the top of the sill and pressing under the fender. Soon the dyke began to brim. The taste of salt-water must have made the otter hungry again, or perhaps he had been waiting for the tide, for he left his playthings and, dropping into the water, went down the dyke towards the marshman's cottage. I crept stealthily along the grassy border of the road, watching the arrowy ripple gleaming with the silver of the thin curved moon. The hillside under the ruined chapel above the village of Branton began to show yellow speckles of light in distant houses. The dyke being deserted (for the brood of ducklings with their hen had been shut up for the night) why then that sudden swirl and commotion in the water by the flag-irises, just where the ducklings had been taken before?

Bubbles broke on the water in strings—big bubbles. Then something heaved glimmering out of the leat, flapping and splashing violently. The noises ceased, and more bubbles came up; the water rocked. Suddenly the splashing increased, and seemed to be moving up and down the leat, breaking the surface of the water. Splashes wetted my face. A considerable struggle was going on there. After a minute there was a new noise—the noise of sappy stalks of the flags being broken. Slap, slap, slap, on the water. I saw streaks and spots of phosphorescence or moon-gleams by the end of the plank. The flapping went on in the meadow beyond the flags, with a sound of biting.

I stood without moving for some minutes, while the biting and squirming went on steadily. My shoes filled with water. The water had spread silently half across the

road. Then the noises ceased. I heard a dull rap, as of
something striking the heavy wooden plank under
water; a strange noise of blowing, a jangle of iron and a
heavy splash, and many bubbles and faint knocking
sounds. The otter had stepped on the plank to drink, and
was trapped.

At last the marshman, having closed *The History of the
Jews*, placed his spectacles in their case, drawn on his
boots, put on his coat, taken his gun off the nails on the
ceiling beam, put it back for a fluke-spearing pronged
fork in the corner, lit the hurricane lamp, said with grim
triumph, "Now us will go vor to see something!" He
was highly pleased that he had outwitted the otter.

"There be no hurry, midear," he said. "Give'n plenty
of time vor to see the water for the last occasion in his
skin."

We stood for a while by the clammer, under the dark
and softly shivering leaves of the willow looming over us
in the lamplight.

The water had receded from the plank when the last
feeble tug came along the brass wire.

The marshman, watched by his dog hopping round
and round on its wooden leg in immense excitement,
pulled up the bundle of gins, and the sagging beast held to
them by a forepaw. It was quite dead; but the marshman
decided to leave it there all night, to make certain.

"I see in the paper," he said, "that a chap up to Lunnon
be giving good money for the best artter skins"—tapping
the spearing handle significantly with his hand.

When it had been dropped in the water again we went a
few paces into the meadow with the lamp, and by its light
we saw a conger eel, thick through as a man's arm, lying
in the grass. The dark living sinuousness was gone from
it; and stooping, we saw that it had been bitten through
the tail. Suddenly I thought it must have come with the
high spring-tide over the sea-wall; and soon afterward,
the keen-nosed otter, following eagerly the scent where it

had squirmed and writhed its way in the grass. The conger had stayed in the dyke, hiding in a drain by the flag-irises, and coming out when the colder salt-water had drifted down.

The marshman carried it back to his cottage, and cut it open, and then stared into my face with amazement and sadness, for within the great eel were the remains of his ducklings.

Laura

"You are not really dying, are you?" asked Amanda.

"I have the doctor's permission to live till Tuesday," said Laura.

"But today is Saturday; this is serious!" gasped Amanda.

"I don't know about it being serious; it is certainly Saturday," said Laura.

"Death is always serious," said Amanda.

"I never said I was going to die. I am presumably going to leave off being Laura, but I shall go on being something. An animal of some kind, I suppose. You see, when one hasn't been very good in the life one has just lived, one reincarnates in some lower organism. And I haven't been very good, when one comes to think of it. I've been petty and mean and vindictive and all that sort of thing when circumstances have seemed to warrant it."

"Circumstances never warrant that sort of thing," said Amanda hastily.

"If you don't mind my saying so," observed Laura, "Egbert is a circumstance that would warrant any amount of that sort of thing. You're married to him—that's different; you've sworn to love, honour and endure him: I haven't."

"I don't see what's wrong with Egbert," protested Amanda.

"Oh, I dare say the wrongness has been on my part," admitted Laura dispassionately; "he has merely been the

164

extenuating circumstance. He made a thin, peevish kind of fuss, for instance, when I took the collie puppies from the farm out for a run the other day."

"They chased his young broods of speckled Sussex and drove two sitting hens off their nests, besides running all over the flower beds. You know how devoted he is to his poultry and garden."

"Anyhow, he needn't have gone on about it for the entire evening, and then have said, 'Let's say no more about it' just when I was beginning to enjoy the discussion. That's where one of my petty vindictive revenges came in," added Laura with an unrepentant chuckle; "I turned the entire family of speckled Sussex into his seedling shed the day after the puppy episode."

"How could you?" exclaimed Amanda.

"It came quite easy," said Laura; "two of the hens pretended to be laying at the time, but I was firm."

"And we thought it was an accident!"

"You see," resumed Laura, "I really have some grounds for supposing that my next incarnation will be in a lower organism. I shall be an animal of some kind. On the other hand, I haven't been a bad sort in my way, so I think I may count on being a nice animal, something elegant and lively, with a love of fun. An otter, perhaps."

"I can't imagine you as an otter," said Amanda.

"Well, I don't suppose you can imagine me as an angel, if it comes to that," said Laura.

Amanda was silent. She couldn't.

"Personally I think an otter life would be rather enjoyable," continued Laura; "salmon to eat all the year round, and the satisfaction of being able to fetch the trout in their own homes without having to wait for hours till they condescend to rise to the fly you've been dangling before them; and an elegant svelte figure—"

"Think of the otter hounds," interposed Amanda; "how dreadful to be hunted and harried and finally worried to death!"

"Rather fun with half the neighbourhood looking on,

and anyhow not worse than this Saturday-to-Tuesday business of dying by inches; and then I should go into something else. If I had been a moderately good otter I suppose I should get back into human shape of some sort; probably something rather primitive—a little, brown, unclothed Nubian boy, I should think."

"I wish you would be serious," sighed Amanda; "you really ought to be if you're only going to live till Tuesday."

As a matter of fact Laura died on Monday.

"So dreadfully upsetting," Amanda complained to her uncle-in-law, Sir Lulworth Quayne. "I've asked quite a lot of people down for golf and fishing, and the rhododendrons are just looking their best."

"Laura always was inconsiderate," said Sir Lulworth; "she was born during Goodwood week, with an Ambassador staying in the house who hated babies."

"She had the maddest kind of ideas," said Amanda; "do you know if there was any insanity in her family?"

"Insanity? No, I never heard of any. Her father lives in West Kensington, but I believe he's sane on all other subjects."

"She had an idea that she was going to be reincarnated as an otter," said Amanda.

"One meets with those ideas of reincarnation so frequently, even in the West," said Sir Lulworth, "that one can hardly set them down as being mad. And Laura was such an unaccountable person in this life that I should not like to lay down definite rules as to what she might be doing in an after state."

"You think she really might have passed into some animal form?" asked Amanda. She was one of those who shape their opinions rather readily from the standpoint of those around them.

Just then Egbert entered the breakfast-room, wearing an air of bereavement that Laura's demise would have been insufficient, in itself, to account for.

"Four of my speckled Sussex have been killed," he

exclaimed; "the very four that were to go to the show on Friday. One of them was dragged away and eaten right in the middle of that new carnation bed that I've been to such trouble and expense over. My best flower bed and my best fowls singled out for destruction; it almost seems as if the brute that did the deed had special knowledge how to be as devastating as possible in a short space of time."

"Was it a fox, do you think?" asked Amanda.

"Sounds more like a polecat," said Sir Lulworth.

"No," said Egbert, "there were marks of webbed feet all over the place, and we followed the tracks down to the stream at the bottom of the garden; evidently an otter."

Amanda looked quickly and furtively across at Sir Lulworth.

Egbert was too agitated to eat any breakfast, and went out to superintend the strengthening of the poultry yard defences.

"I think she might at least have waited till the funeral was over," said Amanda in a scandalized voice.

"It's her own funeral, you know," said Sir Lulworth; "it's a nice point in etiquette how far one ought to show respect to one's own mortal remains."

Disregard for mortuary convention was carried to further lengths next day; during the absence of the family at the funeral ceremony the remaining survivors of the speckled Sussex were massacred. The marauder's line of retreat seemed to have embraced most of the flower beds on the lawn, but the strawberry beds in the lower garden had also suffered.

"I shall get the otter hounds to come here at the earliest possible moment," said Egbert savagely.

"On no account! You can't dream of such a thing!" exclaimed Amanda. "I mean, it wouldn't do, so soon after a funeral in the house."

"It's a case of necessity," said Egbert; "once an otter takes to that sort of thing it won't stop."

"Perhaps it will go elsewhere now that there are no more fowls left," suggested Amanda.

"One would think you wanted to shield the beast," said Egbert.

"There's been so little water in the stream lately," objected Amanda; "It seems hardly sporting to hunt an animal when it has so little chance of taking refuge anywhere."

"Good gracious!" fumed Egbert, "I'm not thinking about sport. I want to have the animal killed as soon as possible."

Even Amanda's opposition weakened when, during church time on the following Sunday, the otter made its way into the house, raided half a salmon from the larder and worried it into scaly fragments on the Persian rug in Egbert's studio.

"We shall have it hiding under our beds and biting pieces out of our feet before long," said Egbert, and from what Amanda knew of this particular otter she felt that the possibility was not a remote one.

On the evening preceding the day fixed for the hunt Amanda spent a solitary hour walking by the banks of the stream, making what she imagined to be hound noises. It was charitably supposed by those who overheard her performance that she was practising for farmyard imitations at the forthcoming village entertainment.

It was her friend and neighbour, Aurora Burret, who brought her news of the day's sport.

"Pity you weren't out; we had quite a good day. We found it at once, in the pool just below your garden."

"Did you—kill?" asked Amanda.

"Rather. A fine she-otter. Your husband got rather badly bitten in trying to 'tail it'. Poor beast, I felt quite sorry for it, it had such a human look in its eyes when it was killed. You'll call me silly, but do you know who the look reminded me of? My dear woman, what is the matter?"

When Amanda had recovered to a certain extent from

168

her attack of nervous prostration Egbert took her to the Nile Valley to recuperate. Change of scenery speedily brought about the desired recovery of health and mental balance. The escapades of an adventurous otter in search of a variation of diet were viewed in their proper light. Amanda's normally placid temperament reasserted itself. Even a hurricane of shouted curses, coming from her husband's dressing-room, in her husband's voice, but hardly in his usual vocabulary, failed to disturb her serenity as she made a leisurely toilet one evening in a Cairo hotel.

"What is the matter? What has happened?" she asked in amused curiosity.

"The little beast has thrown all my clean shirts into the bath! Wait till I catch you, you little—"

"What little beast?" asked Amanda, suppressing a desire to laugh; Egbert's language was so hopelessly inadequate to express his outraged feelings.

"A little beast of a naked brown Nubian boy," spluttered Egbert.

And now Amanda is seriously ill.

The Dragons

DAVID ATTENBOROUGH

The expedition in quest of a dragon has finally reached the Indonesian island of Komodo.

That evening, the boat anchored safely in the bay, we sat in the headman's hut discussing our plans in detail. The headman called the giant lizards *buaja darat*—land crocodiles. There were very many on the island, he told us, so many that sometimes one would wander right into the village to scavenge among the refuse tips. I asked him whether anyone from the village ever hunted them. He shook his head vigorously. *Buaja* were not so good to eat as the wild pigs which were abundant, so why should his men kill them? And in any case, he added, they were dangerous animals. Only a few months ago a man was walking through the bush when he stumbled upon a *buaja* lying motionless in the *alang-alang* grass. The monster had struck with its powerful tail, knocking the man over and numbing his legs so that he was unable to escape. The creature then turned and mauled him with its jaws. His wounds were so severe that he died soon after his comrades found him.

We asked the headman how we could best attract the lizards so that we could take photographs. He was in no doubt.

They have a very keen sense of smell, he told us, and they will come from very long distances to putrefying meat. He would slaughter two goats that night and tomorrow his son would take them to a place on the other side of the bay where the *buaja* were plentiful. All would be well.

I had hoped to be off early, but it took nearly two hours for Haling to prepare himself for the voyage and to collect three other men to help carry all our gear. At last we helped him push his fifteen foot long outrigger canoe down the beach and into the water. We loaded it with our cameras, tripods and recording machines, together with the two goat carcasses slung on a long bamboo.

The sun had already risen above the brown mountains ahead of us as we set out across the bay. The water spurted white over the bamboo outrigger. Haling sat in the stern holding the rope attached to one corner of the rectangular sail, adjusting its trim to suit the varying wind. Soon we were sailing beneath steep rocky cliffs. High up on a ledge above us a splendid fish eagle stood alert, the sun glinting on the chestnut feathers of his mantle.

We landed at the mouth of a valley choked with scrub which ran down from the bare, grass-covered mountains. Haling led us inland, cutting a path through the thorn bushes. We walked for an hour. Here and there we passed a dead tree, its barkless bleached branches riven by the heat of the sun. There was no sign of life except for the chirring of insects and the vociferous screams of parties of sulphur-crested cockatoos which fled ahead of us. It was oppressively hot; a blanket of lowering clouds had spread across the sky, preventing the heat from leaving the baked land.

At last we came to the dry gravelly bed of a stream, as wide and as level as a road; on one side it was overhung by a bank fifteen feet high which was draped with a tangle of roots and lianas. Tall trees grew above, arching over the bed to meet the branches of the trees from the other bank and forming a high spacious tunnel down which the stream-bed curved and disappeared.

Haling stopped and put down the equipment he had been carrying. "Here," he said.

Our first task was to create the smell which we hoped would attract the lizards. The goats' carcasses, already decomposing slightly in the heat, were blown up and swollen as tight as drums. When Sabran slit the underside of each one a foul-smelling gas hissed out. Then he took some of the skin and burnt it on a small wood fire. Haling climbed one of the palms and chopped down a few leaves with which Charles improvised a hide, while Sabran and I staked out the carcasses on the gravelly stream-bed fifteen yards away. This done, we retired behind the palm-leaf screens and began our wait.

Soon it began to rain, the drops pattering gently on the leaves above us. Haling shook his head.

"No good," he said. "*Buaja* no like rain. He stay in his room."

As our shirts got wetter and the rain water trickled down the channel of my back, I began to feel that the *buaja*, on the whole, was more sensible than we were. Charles sealed all his equipment in water-tight bags. The smell of the rotting goats' flesh permeated the air. Soon the rain stopped and we left our hides beneath the dripping trees and sat on the open sandy bed of the stream to dry. Haling gloomily insisted that no *buaja* would leave their lairs until the sun shone and a breeze sprang up to disperse the stench of the goats' meat which hung around us. I lay back miserably on the soft gravel of the stream-bed and shut my eyes.

When I next opened them I realized with surprise that I must have fallen asleep. I looked round and saw that not only Charles, but Sabran, Haling and the other men were also fast asleep, their heads resting in one another's laps or on our equipment boxes. I looked at my watch. It was three o'clock. Although it had stopped raining there was still no sign of a break in the clouds and it seemed very unlikely that the lizards would come to our bait that day. Time, however, was precious. At least we could build a trap which we could leave overnight, so I roused everyone.

The main body of the trap, a roofed rectangle enclosure about ten feet long, was easily constructed. Haling and the other men began to cut strong poles for us from the trees growing on the banks, and Charles and I selected four of the stoutest and drove them into the stream-bed, using a big boulder as our pile-driver. These were our corner posts. Sabran meanwhile had climbed a tall lontar palm and cut down several large fan-shaped leaves. He then took the stems and split, crushed and thrashed them on a boulder to make them pliable. After he had given the resulting fibres a twist, he handed them to us—pieces of strong serviceable string. With them we lashed long horizontal poles between our corner posts, strengthening the structure with uprights where we thought it necessary. At the end of half an hour we had built a long enclosed box open at one end.

Now we had to make a drop-door. This we built of heavy stakes tied together with Sabran's string. The vertical ones were sharpened at the bottom so that when the door fell they would stick deep into the ground, and the lowest horizontal cross-piece overlapped the corner posts inside the trap so that when the door fell it could not be pushed outwards by the dragon—should we ever get one inside. We completed the door by tying a heavy boulder on it with lianas so that it would be difficult to lift once it had fallen.

All that remained to do was to build the triggering device. First we pushed a tall pole through the roof of the trap and drove it into the ground near the enclosed end. Then we planted the feet of two more on either side of the door and tied them in a cross directly above it. We knotted our cord on to the door, raised it, and ran the cord over the angle of the cross-poles to the upright post at the other end of the trap. Instead of keeping the door raised by tying the cord directly on to the post, we tied it on to a small piece of stick about six inches long. Holding the stick upright and close to the post, we twisted two rings of creeper round it and the post, one near its top and one near its bottom. The weight of the door pulled the cord tight and so prevented the rings from slipping down the pole. Then we fastened a smaller piece of cord to the bottom ring, threaded it through the roof of the trap and attached it to a piece of goat's flesh inside.

To test it, I poked a stick through the bars of the cage and jabbed the bait. This tugged the cord attached to the bottom ring and pulled it downwards. The small piece of stick flew loose and the door at the other end dropped with a thud. Our trap worked.

Two last things remained to complete it. First we piled boulders along the sides so that a dragon inside the trap would not be able to insert its nose under the lowest poles and uproot the entire construction. Then we shrouded the closed end with palm-leaves so that the bait could only be seen through the open door.

The three of us then dragged the remainder of the goats' carcasses to the foot of a tree, threw a rope over a projecting branch and hauled them into the air so that they would not be eaten during the night and their smell would spread widely throughout the valley, attracting dragons towards the trap.

We gathered up all our equipment and walked back in the drizzling rain to the canoe.

The sky was cloudless as we sailed across the bay early the next morning. Haling, seated in the stern of the outrigger canoe, smiled and pointed to the sun.

"Good," he said. "Much sun; much smell from goats; many *buaja*."

We landed and set off through the bush as fast as we could. We pushed our way through the undergrowth and emerged on to one of the patches of open savannah. Haling was ahead when suddenly he stopped. "*Buaja*," he called excitedly. I ran up to him and was just in time to see, fifty yards away on the opposite edge of the savan-

174

nah, a moving black shape disappear with a rustle into the thorn bushes. We dashed over to the spot. The reptile itself had vanished but it had left signs behind it. The previous day's rain had collected in wide shallow puddles on the savannah, but the morning sun had dried them, leaving smooth sheets of mud, and the dragon we had glimpsed had walked over one of these leaving a perfect set of tracks.

Its feet had sunk into the mud, its claws leaving deep gashes. A shallow furrow, swaying between the pugmarks, showed where the beast had dragged its tail. From the wide spacing of the footprints and the depth to which they had sunk in the mud, we knew that the dragon we had seen had been a large and heavy one.

We delayed no longer over the tracks but hurried on towards the trap through the dense bush. As we reached a tall dead tree, which I recognized as being within a very short distance of the stream-bed, I was tempted to break into a run, but I checked myself with the thought that to crash noisily through the bush so close to the trap would be a very foolish thing to do, for a dragon might at that very moment be circling the bait. I signalled to Haling and the men to wait. Charles, gripping his camera, Sabran and I picked our way silently through the undergrowth, stepping carefully lest we should tread on a twig and snap it.

I parted the dangling branches of a bush and peered through across the clear emptiness of the river-bed. The trap stood a little below us, a few yards away. Its gate was still hitched high. I felt a wave of disappointment and looked round. There was no sign of a dragon. Cautiously we clambered down to the river-bed and examined the trap. Perhaps our trigger had failed to work and the bait had been taken leaving the trap unsprung. Inside, however, the haunch of goat's meat was still hanging, black with flies. The smooth sand round the trap was unmarked except for our own footsteps.

Sabran returned to fetch the boys with the rest of our

recording and photographic equipment. Charles began to repair the hides we had erected the day before, and I walked farther up the stream-bed to the tree in which we had suspended the major part of our bait. To my delight I saw that the sand beneath was scuffed and disturbed. Without doubt something had been here earlier trying to snatch the bait.

As I untied the rope and lowered the carcasses the smell was almost more than I could stand. These big carcasses were obviously more potent magnets than the bait in the trap, and as our primary task was to film the giant lizards, I dragged the meat to a place on the stream-bed which was in clear view of the cameras in the hide. Then I drove a stout stake deep into the ground and tied them securely to it, so that the dragons would be unable to pull them away into the bush, and, if they wished to eat, would be compelled to do so within easy range of our lenses. That done, I joined Charles and Sabran behind our screen and began to wait.

The sun was shining strongly and shafts of light struck through the gaps in the branches above us, dappling the sand of the river-bed. Although we ourselves were shaded by the bush, it was so hot that sweat poured down us. Charles tied a large handkerchief round his forehead to prevent his perspiration trickling on to the viewfinders of his camera.

After a quarter of an hour my position on the ground became extremely uncomfortable. Noiselessly, I shifted my weight on to my hands, and uncrossed my legs. Next to me, Charles crouched by his camera, the long black lens of which projected between the palm leaves of the screen. Sabran squatted on the other side of him. Even from where we sat, we could smell only too strongly the stench of the bait fifteen yards in front of us. This, however, was encouraging for this smell should attract the dragons.

We had been sitting in absolute silence for over half an hour when there was a rustling noise immediately behind

176

us. Very slowly, so as not to make any noise, I twisted round to tell the boys not to be impatient and to return to the boat. Charles and Sabran remained with their eyes riveted on the bait. I was three-quarters of the way round before I discovered that the noise had not been made by men.

There, facing me, less than four yards away, crouched the dragon.

He was enormous. From the tip of his narrow head to the end of his long keeled tail he measured a full twelve feet. He was so close to us that I could distinguish every beady scale in his hoary black skin which, as if too large for him, hung in long horizontal folds on his flanks and was puckered and wrinkled round his powerful neck. He was standing high on his four bowed legs, his heavy body lifted clear of the ground, his head erect and menacing. The line of his savage mouth curved upwards in a fixed sardonic grin and from between his half-closed jaws an enormous yellow-pink forked tongue slid in and out. There was nothing between us and him but a few very small seedling trees sprouting from the leaf-covered ground. I nudged Charles, who turned, saw the dragon and nudged Sabran. The three of us sat staring at the monster. He stared back.

It flashed across my mind that at least he was in no position to use his main offensive weapon, his tail. Further, if he came towards us both Sabran and I were close to trees and I was sure that I would be able to shin up mine very fast if I had to. Charles, sitting in the middle, was not so well placed.

Except for his long tongue, which he unceasingly flicked in and out, the dragon stood motionless.

For almost a minute none of us moved or spoke. Then Charles laughed softly.

"You know," he whispered, keeping his eyes fixed warily on the monster, "he has probably been standing there for the last ten minutes watching us just as intently and quietly as we have been watching the bait."

The dragon emitted a heavy sigh and slowly splayed his legs, so that his great body sank on to the ground.

"He seems very obliging," I whispered back to Charles. "Why not take his portrait here and now?"

"Can't. The telephoto lens is on the camera and at this distance it would fill the picture with his right nostril."

"Well, let's risk disturbing him and change lens."

Very, very slowly Charles reached in the camera case beside him, took out the stubby wide-angle lens and screwed it into place. He swung the camera round, focused carefully on to the dragon's head and pressed the starting button. The soft whirring of the camera seemed to make an almost deafening noise. The dragon was not in the least concerned but watched us imperiously with his unblinking black eye. It was as though he realized that he was the most powerful beast on Komodo, and that, as king of his island, he feared no other creature. A yellow butterfly fluttered over our heads and settled on his nose. He ignored it. Charles pressed the button again and filmed the butterfly as it flapped into the air, circled and settled again on the dragon's nose.

"This," I muttered, "seems a bit silly. Doesn't the brute understand what we've built the hide for?"

The smell of the bait drifted over to us and it occurred to me that we were sitting in a direct line between the dragon and the bait which had attracted him here.

Just then I heard a noise from the river-bed. I looked behind me and saw a young dragon waddling along the sand towards the bait. It was only about three feet in length and had much brighter markings than the monster close to us. Its tail was banded with dark rings and its forelegs and shoulders were spotted with flecks of dull orange. It walked briskly with a peculiar reptilian gait, twisting its spine sideways and wriggling its hips.

Charles tugged at my sleeve, and without speaking pointed up the stream-bed to our left. Another enormous lizard was advancing towards the bait. It looked even bigger than the one behind us. We were surrounded by these wonderful creatures.

The dragon behind us recalled our attention by emitting another deep sigh. He flexed his splayed legs and heaved his body off the ground. He took a few steps forward, turned and slowly stalked round us. We followed him with our eyes. He approached the bank and slithered down it. Charles followed him round with the camera until he was able to swing it back into its original position.

The tension snapped and we all dissolved into smothered delighted laughter.

All three reptiles were now feeding in front of us. Savagely they tore at the goat's flesh. The biggest beast seized one of the goat's legs in his jaws. He was so large that I had to remind myself that what he was treating as a single mouthful was in fact the complete leg of a full-grown goat. Bracing his feet far apart, he began ripping at the carcass with powerful backward jerks of his entire body. If the bait had not been securely tied to the stake, I was sure he would with ease have dragged the entire carcass away to the forest. Charles filmed feverishly, and soon had exhausted all the film in his magazines.

"What about some still photographs?" he whispered.

This was my responsibility, but my camera had not the powerful lenses of the ciné camera and I should have to get much closer if I were to obtain good photographs.

Slowly I straightened up behind the hide and stepped out beside it. I took two cautious steps forward and took a photograph. The dragons continued feeding without so much as a glance in my direction. I took another step forward and another photograph. Soon I had exposed all the film in my camera and was standing nonplussed in the middle of the open river-bed within two yards of the monsters. There was nothing else to do but to go back to the hide and reload. Though the dragons seemed preoccupied with their meal, I did not risk turning my back on them as I returned slowly to the hide.

With a new film in my camera I advanced more boldly and did not begin photographing until I was within six feet of them. I inched closer and closer. Eventually, I was standing with my feet touching the forelegs of the goat carcass. I reached inside my pocket and took out a supplementary portrait lens for my camera. The big dragon three feet away withdrew his head from inside the goat's ribs with a piece of flesh in his mouth. He straightened up, and with a few convulsive snappings of his jaws, he gulped it down. He remained in this position for a few seconds looking squarely at the camera. I knelt and took his photograph. Then he once more lowered his head and began wrenching off another mouthful.

I retreated to Charles and Sabran for a consultation. Obviously, a close approach would not frighten the creatures away. We decided to try noise. The three of us stood up and shouted. The dragons ignored us totally. Only when we rushed together from the hide towards them did they interrupt their meal. The two big ones turned and lumbered up the bank and off into the bush. The little one, however, scuttled straight down the river-bed. I chased after it, running as fast as I could, in an attempt to catch it with my hands. It outpaced me, and as it came to a dip in the bank it raced up and disappeared into the undergrowth.

I returned panting and helped Charles and Sabran to hoist the carcasses into a tree twenty yards away from the trap and then once more we waited. I was fearful that having frightened the dragons once they would not return. But I need not have worried; within ten minutes the big one reappeared on the bank opposite us. For some time he snuffled round the patch of sand where the bait had been lying, protruding his great tongue and tasting the last remnants of the smell in the air. He seemed mystified. He cast around, his head in the air, seeking the meal of which he had been robbed. Then he set off ponderously along the river-bed, but to our dismay walked straight past our trap towards the suspended bait.

As he approached it, we realized that we had not tied it sufficiently high, for the creature reared up on its hind legs, using its enormous muscular tail as a counterbalance, and with a downward sweep of his foreleg snatched down a tangle of the goat's innards. He wolfed it immediately, but the end of a long rope of intestine hung down from the angle of his jaw. This displeased him and for a few minutes he tried to paw it off, but without success.

He lumbered along the stream-bed, back towards the trap, shaking his head angrily. As he reached a large boulder, he stopped, rasped his scaly cheek against it and at last wiped his jaws clean. Now he was near the trap. The smell of the bait inside filtered into his nostrils and he turned aside from his path to investigate. Sensing accurately the direction from which the smell came, he moved directly to the closed end of the trap and with savage impatient swipes of his forelegs he ripped aside the palm-leaf shroud, exposing the wooden bars. He forced his blunt snout between two of the poles and heaved with his powerful neck. To our relief, the lianas binding the bars together held firm. Baulked, he at last approached the door. With maddening caution, he looked inside. He took three steps forward. All we could see of him was his hind-legs and his enormous tail. For an interminable time he made no movement. At last he went further inside and disappeared entirely from view. Suddenly there was a click, the trigger rope flew loose and the gate thudded down, burying its sharpened stakes deep into the sand.

Exultantly we ran forward. We grabbed boulders and piled them against the trap door. The dragon peered at us superciliously, flicking his forked tongue through the bars. We could hardly believe that we had achieved the objective of our four months' trip, that in spite of all our difficulties we had at last succeeded in catching a specimen of the largest lizard in the world. We sat on the sand looking at our prize and smiling breathlessly at one

another. In the end we were refused permission to export
the dragon. This was a great and unexpected blow to us,
but we were allowed to take the rest of our animals back
to London.

In one way I was not sorry that we had to leave the
dragon behind. He would, I am sure, have been happy
and healthy in the large heated enclosures of London's
Reptile House, but he could never have appeared to
anyone else as he did to us that day on Komodo when we
turned round to see him a few feet away, majestic and
magnificent in his own forest.

Home Life of A Holy Cat

ARTHUR WEIGALL

One summer during a heat wave, when the temperature in the shade of my veranda in Luxor was a hundred and twenty-five degrees Fahrenheit, I went down to cooler Lower Egypt to pay a visit to an English friend of mine stationed at Zagazig, the native city which stands beside the ruins of ancient Bubastis.

He was about to leave Egypt and asked me whether I would like to have his cat, a dignified, mystical-minded, long-legged, small-headed, green-eyed female, whose orange-yellow hair, marked with greyish-black stripes in tabby pattern, was so short that she gave the impression of being naked—an impression, however, which did not in any way detract from her air of virginal chastity.

Her name was Basta, and though her more recent ancestors had lived wild amongst the ruins, she was so obviously a descendant of the holy cats of ancient times, who were incarnations of the goddess Basta, that I thought it only right to accept the offer and take her up to Luxor to live with me. To be the expert in charge of Egyptian antiquities and not have an ancient Egyptian cat to give an air of mystery to my headquarters had, indeed, always seemed to me to be somewhat wanting in showmanship on my part.

Thus it came about that on my departure I drove off to the railway station with the usually dignified Basta bumping around and uttering unearthly howls inside a cardboard hatbox, in the side of which I had cut a small

183

round hole for ventilation. The people in the street and on the station platform seemed to be under the impression that the noises were digestive and that I was in dire need of a doctor; and it was a great relief to my embarrassment when the hot and panting train steamed into Luxor.

Fortunately I found myself alone in the compartment, and the hatbox on the seat at my side had begun to cause me less anxiety, when suddenly Basta was seized with a sort of religious frenzy. The box rocked about, and presently out through the air-hole came a long, snake-like paw which waved weirdly to and fro in space for a moment and then was withdrawn, its place being taken by a pink nose which pushed itself outward with such frantic force that the sides of the hole gave way, and out burst the entire sandy, sacred head.

She then began to choke, for the cardboard was pressing tightly around her neck; and to save her from strangulation I was obliged to tear the aperture open, whereupon she wriggled out, leaped in divine frenzy up the side of the carriage, and prostrated herself on the network of the baggage-rack, where her hysteria caused her to lose all control of her internal arrangements, and if I say modestly that she was overcome with nausea I shall be telling but a part of the dreadful tale.

The rest of the journey was like a bad dream; but at the Cairo terminus, where I had to change into the night express for Luxor, I got the help of a native policeman who secured a large laundry basket from the sleeping-car department, and after a prolonged struggle, during which the train was shunted into a distant siding, we imprisoned the struggling Basta again.

The perspiring policeman and I then carried the basket at a run along the tracks back to the station in the sweltering heat of the late afternoon, and I just managed to catch my train; but during this second part of my journey Basta travelled in the baggage van, whence, in the hot and silent night, whenever we were at a standstill, her appalling incantations came drifting to my ears.

Home Life of a Holy Cat

I opened the basket in an unfurnished spare-room in
my house, and like a flash Basta was up the bare wall and
on to the curtain pole above the window. There she
remained all day, in a sort of mystic trance; but at sunset
the saucer of milk and a plate of fish which I had provided
for her at last enticed her down, and in the end she
reconciled herself to her new surroundings and indicated
by her behaviour that she was willing to accept my house
as her earthly temple.

With Pedro, my pariah dog, there was not the slightest
trouble; he had no strong feelings about cats, and she on
her part graciously deigned to acknowledge his
status—as, I believe, is generally the case in native house-
holds. She sometimes condescended to visit my horse
and donkey in their stalls; and for Laura, my camel, she
quickly developed a real regard, often sleeping for hours
in her stable.

I was not worried as to how she would treat the chickens and pigeons, because her former owner at Zagazig
had insisted upon her respecting his hen-coop and
pigeon-cote; but I was a little anxious about the ducks,
for she had not previously known any, and in ancient
times her ancestors used to be trained to hunt wild geese
and ducks and were fed with *pâté de foie gras*, or whatever
it was called then, on holy days and anniversaries.

In a corner of the garden I had made a miniature duck
pond which was sunk rather deeply in the ground and
down to which I had cut a narrow, steeply sloping passage, or gangway. During the day, after the ducks had
been up and down this slope several times, the surface
used to become wet and slippery, and the ducks, having
waddled down the first few inches, were forced to
toboggan down the rest of it on their tails, with their two
feet sticking out in front of them and their heads well up.

Basta was always fascinated by this slide and by the
splash at the bottom, and used to sit and watch it all for
hours, which made me think at first she would one day
spring at one of them; but she never did. Field mice, and

water rats down by the Nile, were her only prey; and in connection with the former I may mention a curious occurrence.

One hot night I was sitting smoking my pipe on the veranda when my attention was attracted by two mice which had crept into the patch of brilliant moonlight before my feet and were boldly nibbling some crumbs left over from a biscuit thrown to Pedro earlier in the evening. I watched them silently for a while and did not notice that Basta had seen them and was preparing to spring, nor did I observe a large white owl sitting aloft amongst the overhanging roses and also preparing to pounce.

Suddenly, and precisely at the same moment, the owl shot down on the mice from above and Basta leaped at them from beside me. There was a collision and a wild scuffle; fur and feathers flew; I fell out of my chair; and then the owl made off screeching in one direction and the cat dashed away in the other; while the mice, practically clinging to each other, remained for a moment or so too terrified to move.

During the early days of her residence in Luxor, Basta often used to go down to the edge of the Nile to fish with her paw; but she never caught anything, and in the end she got a fright and gave it up. I was sitting by the river watching her trying to catch one of a little shoal of small fish which were sunning themselves in the shallow water when there came swimming into view a twelve- or fourteen-inch fish which I recognized (by its whiskers and the absence of a dorsal fin) as the electric catfish, pretty common in the Nile—a strange creature able to give you an electric shock like hitting your funny-bone.

These fish obtain their food in a curious way: they hang round any shoal of small fry engaged in feeding, and then glide quietly into their midst and throw out this electric shock, whereupon the little fellows are all sick to the stomach, and the big fellow gets their disgorged dinners.

I was just waiting to see this happen with my own eyes—for it had always seemed a bit far-fetched—when Basta made a dart at the intruder with her paw and got a shock. She uttered a yowl as though somebody had trodden on her and leaped high in the air; and never again did she put her foot near the water. She was content after that with our daily offering of fish brought from the market and fried for her like a burnt sacrifice.

Basta had a most unearthly voice, and when she was feeling emotional would let out a wail which at first was like the crying of a phantom baby, and then became the tuneless song of a lunatic, and finally developed into the blood-curdling howl of a soul in torment. And when she spat, the percussion was like that of a spring gun.

There were some wild cats, or, rather, domestic cats who, like Basta's own forebears, had taken to a wild life, living in a grove of trees beside the river just beyond my garden wall; and it was generally the proximity of one of these which started her off; but sometimes the outburst was caused by her own unfathomable thoughts as she went her mysterious ways in the darkness of the night.

I think she must have been clairvoyant, for she often seemed to be seeing things not visible to me. Sometimes, perhaps when she was cleaning fish or mouse from her face, she would pause with one foot off the ground and stare in front of her, and then back away with bristling hair or go forward with friendly little mewing noises; and sometimes she would leap off a chair or sofa, her tail lashing and her green eyes dilated. But it may have been worms.

Once I saw her standing absolutely rigid and tense on the lawn, staring at the rising moon; and then all of a sudden she did a sort of dance such as cats sometimes do when they are playing with other cats. But there was no other cat, and, anyway, Basta never played; she never forgot that she was a holy cat.

Her chaste hauteur was so great that she would not move out of the way when people were walking about, and many a time her demoniacal shriek and perhaps a crash of breaking glass informed the household that somebody had tripped over her. It was astonishing, however, how quickly she recovered her dignity and how well she maintained the pretence that whatever happened to her was at her own celestial wish and was not our doing.

If I called her she would pretend not to hear, but would come a few moments later when it could appear that she had thought of doing so first; and if I lifted her off a chair she would jump back on to it and then descend with dignity as though of her own free will. But in this, of course, she was more like a woman than a divinity.

The Egyptian cat is a domesticated species of the African wildcat, and no doubt its strange behaviour and its weird voice were the cause of it being regarded as sacred in ancient times; but, although the old gods and their worship have been forgotten these many centuries, the traditional sanctity of the race has survived.

Modern Egyptians think it unlucky to hurt a cat, and in the native quarters of Cairo and other cities hundreds of cats are daily fed at the expense of benevolent citizens. They say that they do this because cats are so useful to mankind in killing off mice and other pests; but actually it is an unrecognized survival of the old beliefs.

In the old days of the Pharaohs, when a cat died the men of the household shaved off their eyebrows and sat around wailing and rocking themselves to and fro in simulated anguish. The body was embalmed and buried with solemn rites in the local cats' cemetery, or was sent down to Bubastis to rest in the shadow of the temple of their patron goddess. I myself have dug up hundreds of mummified cats; and once, when I had a couple of dozen of the best specimens standing on my own veranda waiting to be dispatched to the Cairo Museum, Basta was most excited about it, and walked around sniffing at them all day. They certainly smelled awful.

On my lawn there was a square slab of stone which had

once been the top of an altar dedicated to the sun god, but was now used as a sort of low garden table; and sometimes when she had caught a mouse she used to deposit the chewed corpse upon this slab—nobody could think why, unless, as I always told people, she was really making an offering to the sun. It was most mysterious of her; but it led once to a very unfortunate episode.

A famous French antiquarian, who was paying a polite call, was sitting with me beside this sacred stone, drinking afternoon tea and eating fresh dates, when Basta appeared on the scene with a small dead mouse in her mouth, which in her usual way she deposited upon the slab—only on this occasion she laid it on my guest's plate, which was standing on the slab.

We were talking at the moment and did not see her do this, and anyhow, the Frenchman was as blind as a bat; and, of course, as luck would have it, he immediately picked up the wet, mole-coloured mouse instead of a ripe brown date, and the thing had almost gone into his mouth before he saw what it was and, with a yell, flung it into the air.

It fell into his upturned sun helmet, which was lying on the grass beside him; but he did not see where it had gone, and jumping angrily to his feet in the momentary belief that I had played a schoolboy joke on him, he snatched up his helmet and was in the act of putting it on his head when the mouse tumbled out on to the front of his shirt and slipped down inside his buttoned jacket.

At this he went more or less mad, danced about, shook himself, and finally trod on Basta, who completed his frenzy by uttering a fiendish howl and digging her claws into his leg. The dead mouse, I am glad to say, fell on to the grass during the dance without passing through his roomy trousers, as I had feared it might, and Basta, recovering her dignity, picked it up and walked off with it.

It is a remarkable fact that during the five or six years she spent with me she showed no desire to be anything

189

but a spinster all her life, and when I arranged a marriage for her she displayed such dignified but violent antipathy towards the bridegroom that the match was a failure. In the end, however, she fell in love with one of the wild cats who lived among the trees beyond my wall, and nothing could prevent her from going off to visit him from time to time, generally at dead of night.

He did not care a hoot about her sanctity, and she was feminine enough to enjoy the novelty of being roughly treated. I never actually saw him, for he did not venture into the garden, but I used to hear him knocking her about outside my gates; and when she came home, scratched and bitten and muttering something about holy cats, it was plain that she was desperately happy. She licked her wounds, indeed, with voluptuous satisfaction.

A dreadful change came over her. She lost her precious dignity and was restless and inclined to be savage; her digestion played embarrassing tricks on her; and once she mortally offended Laura by clawing her nose. There was a new glint in her green eyes as she watched the ducks sliding into the pond; the pigeons interested her for the first time; and for the first time, too, she *ate* the mice she had caught.

Then she began to disappear for a whole day or night at a time, and once when I went in search of her amongst the trees outside and found her sharpening her claws on a branch above my head, she put her ears back and hissed at me until I could see every one of her teeth and half-way down her pink throat. I tried by every method to keep her at home when she came back, but it was all in vain, and at last she left me for ever.

Weeks afterward I caught sight of her once again amongst the trees, and it was evident that she was soon to become a mother. She gave me a friendly little mew this time, but she would not let me touch her; and presently she slipped away into the undergrowth. I never knew what became of her.

The Cow that would never get up n'more

JAMES HERRIOT

I could see that Mr Handshaw didn't believe a word I was saying. He looked down at his cow and his mouth tightened into a stubborn line.

"Broken pelvis? You're trying to tell me she'll never get up n'more? Why, look at her chewing her cud! I'll tell you this, young man—me dad would've soon got her up if he'd been alive today."

I had been a veterinary surgeon for a year now and I had learned a few things. One of them was that farmers weren't easy men to convince—especially Yorkshire Dalesmen.

And that bit about his dad. Mr Handshaw was in his fifties and I suppose there was something touching about his faith in his late father's skill and judgement. But I could have done very nicely without it.

It had acted as an additional irritant in a case in which I felt I had troubles enough. Because there are few things which get more deeply under a vet's skin than a cow which won't get up. To the layman it may seem strange that an animal can be apparently cured of its original ailment and yet be unable to rise from the floor, but it happens. And it can be appreciated that a completely recumbent milk cow has no future.

The case had started when my boss, Siegfried Farnon, who owned the practice in the little Dales market town of Darrowby, sent me to a milk fever. This suddenly occurring calcium deficiency attacks high yielding animals just after calving and causes collapse and progressive coma. When I first saw Mr Handshaw's cow she was stretched out motionless on her side, and I had to look carefully to make sure she wasn't dead.

But I got out my bottles of calcium with an airy confidence because I had been lucky enough to qualify just about the time when the profession had finally got on top of this hitherto fatal condition. The breakthrough had come many years earlier with inflation of the udder and I still carried a little blowing-up outfit around with me (the farmers used bicycle pumps), but with the advent of calcium therapy one could bask in a cheap glory by jerking an animal back from imminent death within minutes. The skill required was minimal but it looked very very good.

By the time I had injected the two bottles—one into the vein, the other under the skin—and Mr Handshaw had helped me roll the cow on to her chest the improvement was already obvious; she was looking about her and shaking her head as if wondering where she had been for the last few hours. I felt sure that if I had had the time to hang about for a bit I could see her on her feet. But other jobs were waiting.

"Give me a ring if she isn't up by dinner time," I said, but it was a formality. I was pretty sure I wouldn't be seeing her again.

When the farmer rang at midday to say she was still down it was just a pinprick. Some cases needed an extra bottle—it would be all right. I went out and injected her again.

I wasn't really worried when I learned she hadn't got up the following day, but Mr Handshaw, hands deep in pockets, shoulders hunched as he stood over his cow, was grievously disappointed at my lack of success.

"It's time t'awd bitch was up. She's doin' no good laid there. Surely there's summat you can do. I poured a bottle of water into her lug this morning but even that hasn't shifted her."

"You what?"

"Poured some cold water down her lug 'ole. Me dad used to get 'em up that way and he was a very clever man with stock was me dad."

"I've no doubt he was," I said primly. "But I really think another injection is more likely to help her."

The farmer watched glumly as I ran yet another bottle of calcium under the skin. The procedure had lost its magic for him.

As I put the apparatus away I did my best to be hearty. "I shouldn't worry. A lot of them stay down for a day or two—you'll probably find her walking about in the morning."

The phone rang just before breakfast and my stomach contracted sharply as I heard Mr Handshaw's voice. It was heavy with gloom. "Well, she's no different. Lyin' there eating her 'ead off, but never offers to rise. What are you going to do now?"

What indeed, I thought as I drove out to the farm. The cow had been down for forty-eight hours now—I didn't like it a bit.

The farmer went into the attack immediately. "Me dad allus used to say they had a worm in the tail when they stayed down like this. He said if you cut tail end off it did the trick."

My spirits sagged lower. I had had trouble with this myth before. The insidious thing was that the people who still practised this relic of barbarism could often claim that it worked because, after the end of the tail had been chopped off, the pain of the stump touching the ground forced many a sulky cow to scramble to her feet.

"There's no such thing as worm in the tail, Mr Handshaw," I said. "And don't you think it's a cruel business, cutting off a cow's tail? I hear the RSPCA had a man in court last week over a job like that."

The farmer narrowed his eyes. Clearly he thought I was hedging. "Well, if you won't do that, what the

193

hangment are you going to do? We've got to get this cow up somehow."

I took a deep breath. "Well, I'm sure she's got over the milk fever because she's eating well and looks quite happy. It must be a touch of posterior paralysis that's keeping her down. There's no point in giving her any more calcium so I'm going to try this stimulant injection." I filled the syringe with a feeling of doom. I hadn't a scrap of faith in the stimulant injection but I just couldn't do nothing. I was scraping the barrel out now.

I was turning to go when Mr Handshaw called after me. "Hey, Mister, I remember summat else me dad used to do. Shout in their lugs. He got many a cow up that way. I'm not very strong in the voice—how about you having a go?"

It was a bit late to stand on my dignity. I went over to the animal and seized her by the ear. Inflating my lungs to the utmost I bent down and bawled wildly into the hairy depths. The cow stopped chewing for a moment and looked at me inquiringly, then her eyes drooped and she returned contentedly to her cudding. "We'll give her another day," I said wearily. "And if she's still down tomorrow we'll have a go at lifting her. Could you get a few of the neighbours to give us a hand?"

Driving round my other cases that day I felt tied up inside with sheer frustration. Damn and blast the thing! What the hell was keeping her down? And what else could I do? This was 1938 and my resources were limited. Thirty years later there are still milk fever cows which won't get up but the vet has a much wider armoury if the calcium has failed to do the job. The excellent Bagshaw hoist which clamps on to the pelvis and raises the animal in a natural manner, the phosphorus injections, even the electric goad which administers a swift shock when applied to the rump and sends many a comfortably ensconced cow leaping to her feet with an offended bellow.

As I expected, the following day brought no change

194

and as I got out of the car in Mr Handshaw's yard I was surrounded by a group of his neighbours. They were in festive mood, grinning, confident, full of helpful advice as farmers always are with somebody else's animals.

There was much laughter and legpulling as we drew sacks under the cow's body and a flood of weird suggestions to which I tried to close my ears. When we all finally gave a concerted heave and lifted her up, the result was predictable; she just hung there placidly with her legs dangling whilst her owner leaned against the wall watching us with deepening gloom.

After a lot of puffing and grunting we lowered the inert body and everybody looked at me for the next move. I was hunting round desperately in my mind when Mr Handshaw piped up again.

"Me dad used to say a strange dog would allus get a cow up."

There were murmurs of assent from the assembled farmers and immediate offers of dogs. I tried to point out that one would be enough but my authority had dwindled and anyway everybody seemed anxious to demonstrate their dog's cow-raising potential. There was a sudden excited exodus and even Mr Smedley the village shopkeeper pedalled off at frantic speed for his border terrier. It seemed only minutes before the byre was alive with snapping, snarling curs but the cow ignored them all except to wave her horns warningly at the ones which came too close.

The flash-point came when Mr Handshaw's own dog came in from the fields where he had been helping to round up the sheep. He was a skinny, hard-bitten little creature with lightning reflexes and a short temper. He stalked, stiff-legged and bristling, into the byre, took a single astounded look at the pack of foreigners on his territory and flew into action with silent venom.

Within seconds the finest dog fight I had ever seen was in full swing and I stood back and surveyed the scene with a feeling of being completely superfluous. The yells

195

of the farmers rose above the enraged yapping and growling. One intrepid man leaped into the mêlée and reappeared with a tiny Jack Russell hanging on 'determinedly to the heel of his wellington boot. Mr Reynolds of Clover Hill was rubbing the cow's tail between two short sticks and shouting "Cush! Cush!" and as I watched helplessly a total stranger tugged at my sleeve and whispered: "Hasta tried a teaspoonful of Jeyes' Fluid in a pint of old beer every two hours?"

It seemed to me that all the forces of black magic had broken through and were engulfing me and that my slender resources of science had no chance of shoring up the dyke. I don't know how I heard the creaking sound above the din—probably because I was bending low over Mr Reynolds in an attempt to persuade him to desist from his tail rubbing. But at that moment the cow shifted her position slightly and I distinctly heard it. It came from the pelvis.

It took me some time to attract attention—I think everybody had forgotten I was there—but finally the dogs were separated and secured with innumerable lengths of binder twine, everybody stopped shouting, Mr Reynolds was pulled away from the tail and I had the stage.

I addressed myself to Mr Handshaw. "Would you get me a bucket of hot water, some soap and a towel, please."

He trailed off, grumbling, as though he didn't expect much from the new gambit. My stock was definitely low.

I stripped off my jacket, soaped my arms and pushed a hand into the cow's rectum until I felt the hard bone of the pubis. Gripping it through the wall of the rectum I looked up at my audience. "Will two of you get hold of the hook bones and rock the cow gently from side to side."

Yes, there it was again, no mistake about it. I could both hear and feel it—a looseness, a faint creaking, almost a grating.

196

I got up and washed my arm. "Well, I know why your cow won't get up—she has a broken pelvis. Probably did it during the first night when she was staggering about with the milk fever. I should think the nerves are damaged too. It's hopeless, I'm afraid." Even though I was dispensing bad news it was a relief to come up with something rational.

Mr Handshaw stared at me. "Hopeless? How's that?"

"I'm sorry," I said, "but that's how it is. The only thing you can do is get her off to the butcher. She has no power in her hind legs. She'll never get up again."

That was when Mr Handshaw really blew his top and started a lengthy speech. He wasn't really unpleasant or abusive but firmly pointed out my shortcomings and bemoaned again the tragic fact that his dad was not there to put everything right. The other farmers stood in a wide-eyed ring, enjoying every word.

At the end I took myself off. There was nothing more I could do and anyway Mr Handshaw would have to come round to my way of thinking. Time would prove me right.

I thought of that cow as soon as I awoke next morning. It hadn't been a happy episode but at least I did feel a certain peace in the knowledge that there was no hope. There was nothing more to worry about.

I was surprised when I heard Mr Handshaw's voice on the phone so soon. I had thought it would take him two or three days to realize he was wrong.

"Is that Mr Herriot? Aye, well, good mornin' to you. I'm just ringing to tell you that me cow's up on her legs and doing fine."

I gripped the receiver tightly with both hands.

"What? What's that you say?"

"I said me cow's up. Found her walking about byre this morning, fit as a fiddle. You'd think there's never been owt the matter with her." He paused for a few moments then spoke with grave deliberation like a disapproving schoolmaster. "And you stood there and looked at me and said she'd never get up n'more."

"But ... but ..."

"Ah, you're wondering how I did it? Well, I just happened to remember another old trick of me dad's. I went round to t'butcher and got a fresh-killed sheep skin and put it on her back. Had her up in no time—you'll 'ave to come round and see her. Wonderful man was me dad."

Blindly I made my way into the dining-room. I had to consult my boss about this. Siegfried's sleep had been broken by a 3 a.m. calving and he looked a lot older than his thirty-odd years. He listened in silence as he finished his breakfast then pushed away his plate and poured a last cup of coffee. "Hard luck, James. The old sheep skin, eh? Funny thing—you've been in the Dales over a year now and never come across that one. Suppose it must be going out of fashion a bit now but you know it has a grain of sense behind it like a lot of these old remedies. You can imagine there's a lot of heat generated under a fresh sheep skin and it acts like a great hot poultice on the back—really tickles them up after a while, and if a cow is lying there out of sheer cussedness she'll often get up just to get rid of it."

"But damn it, how about the broken pelvis? I tell you it was creaking and wobbling all over the place!"

"Well, James, you're not the first to have been caught that way. Sometimes the pelvic ligaments don't tighten up for a few days after calving and you get this effect."

"Oh God," I moaned, staring down at the table cloth. "What a bloody mess I've made of the whole thing."

"Oh, you haven't really." Siegfried lit a cigarette and leaned back in his chair. "That old cow was probably toying with the idea of getting up for a walk just when old Handshaw dumped the skin on her back. She could just as easily have done it after one of your injections and then you'd have got credit. Don't you remember what I told you when you first came here? There's a very fine dividing line between looking a real smart vet on the one hand and an immortal fool on the other. This sort of thing happens to us all, so forget it, James."

But forgetting wasn't so easy. That cow became a celebrity in the district. Mr Handshaw showed her with pride to the postman, the policeman, corn merchants, lorry drivers, fertilizer salesmen, Ministry of Agriculture officials and they all told me about it frequently with pleased smiles. Mr Handshaw's speech was always the same, delivered, they said, in ringing, triumphant tones:

"There's the cow that Mr Herriot said would never get up n'more!"

I'm sure there was no malice behind the farmer's actions. He had put one over on the young clever-pants vet and nobody could blame him for preening himself a little. And in a way I did that cow a good turn; I considerably extended her life span because Mr Handshaw kept her long beyond her normal working period just as an exhibit. Years after she had stopped giving more than a couple of gallons of milk a day she was still grazing happily in the field by the roadside.

She had one curiously upturned horn and was easy to recognize. I often pulled up my car and looked wistfully over the wall at the cow that would never get up n'more.

Concerning Cats

W. H. HUDSON

... And here I recall an old story of a cat (an immortal puss) who only hunted pigeons. This tells that Sir Henry Wyatt was imprisoned in the Tower of London by Richard III, and was cruelly treated, having no bed to sleep on in his cell and scarcely food enough to keep him alive. One winter night, when he was half dead with cold, a cat appeared in his cell, having come down the chimney, and was very friendly, and slept curled up on his chest, thus keeping him warm all night. In the morning it vanished up the chimney, but appeared later with a pigeon, which it gave to Sir Henry, and then again departed. When the jailer appeared and repeated that he durst not bring more than the few morsels of food provided, Sir Henry then asked: "Wilt thou dress any I provide?" This the jailer promised to do, for he pitied his prisoner, and taking the pigeon had it dressed and cooked for him. The cat continued bringing pigeons every day, and the jailer, thinking they were sent miraculously, continued to cook them, so that Sir Henry fared well, despite the order which Richard gave later, that no food at all was to be provided. He was getting impatient of his prisoner's power to keep alive on very little food, and he didn't want to behead him—he wanted him to die naturally. Thus in the end Sir Henry outlived the tyrant and was set free, and the family preserve the story to this day. It is classed as folk-lore, but there is no reason to prevent one from accepting it as literal truth.

The Seal Man

JOHN MASEFIELD

"The seals is pretty when they do be playing," said the old woman. "Ah, I seen them frisking their tails till you'd think it was rocks with the seas beating on them, the time the storm's on. I seen the merrows of the sea sitting yonder on the dark stone, and they had crowns on them, and they were laughing. The merrows is not good; it's not good to see too many of them. They are beautiful like young men in their shirts playing hurley. They're as beautiful as anything you would be seeing in Americkey or Australeyey, or any place. The seals is beautiful too, going through the water in the young of the day; but they're not so beautiful as them. The seals is no good either. It's a great curse keeps them the way they are, not able to live either in the sea or on the land.

"One time there was a man of the O'Donnells came here, and he was a bad man. A saint in Heaven would have been bothered to find good in him. He died of the fever that came before the Famine. I was a girl then; and if you'd seen the people in them times; there wasn't enough to bury them. The pigs used to eat them in the loanings. And their mouths would be all green where they'd eaten grass from want of food. If you'd seen the houses there was then, indeed, you'd think the place bewitched. But the cabins is all fell in, like wonder, and there's no dancing or fiddling, or anything at all, and all of my friends is gone to Americkey or Australeyey; I've no one at all to bury me, unless it's that humpy one who comes here, and she's as proud as a Jew. She's no cause to be proud, with a hump on her; her father was just a poor man, same as any.

"This O'Donnell I was telling you. My father was at his wake. And they'd the candles lit, and they were drinking putcheen. My father was nearest the door, and a fear took him, and he got up, with his glass in his hand, and he cried out: 'There's something here is not good.' And another of them said: 'There's something here that wants to get out.' And another said: 'It's himself wants to go out into the dark night.' And another said: 'For the love of God, open the door.' So my father flung the door open; and, outside, the moon shone down to the sea. And the corpse of the O'Donnell was all blue, and it got up with the sheet knotted on it, and walked out without leaving a track. So they followed it, saying their prayers to Almighty God, and it walked on down to the sea. And when it came to the edge of the sea, the sea was like a flame before it. And it bowed there, three times; and each time it rose up it screamed. And all the seals, and all the merrows, and all them that's under the tides, they came up to welcome it. They called out to the corpse and laughed; and the corpse laughed back, and fell on to the sand. My father and the other men saw the wraith pass from it, into the water, as it fell. It was like a little black boy, laughing, with great long arms on him. It was all bald and black; and its hands moved like he was tickling someone.

"And after that the priest had him buried, like they buried the Old Ones; but the wraith passed into a bull seal. You would be feared to see the like of the bull seal. There was a man of the O'Kanes fired a blessed shilling at him, and the seal roared up at him and tore his arms across. There was marks like black stars on him after till he died. And the bull seal walked like a man at the change of the moon, like a big, tall, handsome man stepping the roads. You'd be feared, sir, if you saw the like. He set his eyes on young Norah O'Hara. Lovely she was. She'd little ways, sir, would draw the heart out of an old bachelor. Wasn't it a great curse he should take her when there was old hags the like of Mary that had no more beauty than a withered broom that you wouldn't be bothered to mend or a done-out old gather-up of a duck that a hungry dog would blush to be biting? Still, he took Norah.

"She had a little son, and the little son was a seal-man; the priest wouldn't sign him with the cross. When Norah died he used always to be going to the sea; he would always be swimming. He'd little soft brown hair, like a seal's, the prettiest you would be seeing. He used to talk to the seals. My father was coming home one night from Carnmore, and he saw the little seal-man in the sea; and the seals were playing with him, singing songs. But my father was feared to hear; he ran away. They stoned the seal-man, whiles, after that; but whiles they didn't stone it. They had a kindness for it, although it had no holy water on it. It was a very young thing to be walking the world, and it was a beautiful wee thing, with its eyes so pretty; so it grew up to be a man.

"Them that live in the water, they have ways of calling people. Them who pass this seal-man, they felt the call in their hearts. Indeed, if you passed the seal-man, stepping the roads, you would get a queer twist from the way he looked at you. And he set his love on a young girl of the O'Keefe's, a little young girl with no more in her than the flower on its stalk. You would see them in the loanings coming home, or in the bright of the day going. There was a strong love was on them two young things; it was like the love of the Old Ones that took nine deaths to kill. They would be telling Kate it was not right she should set her love on one who wasn't like ourselves; but there's few indeed is the young'll listen. They are all for pleasure, all for pleasure, before they are withered old hags, the like of my sister Mary. And at last they shut her up at home, to keep her from seeing him. And he came by her cabin to the west of the road, calling. There was a strong love came up in her at that, and she put down her sewing on the table, and 'Mother,' she says, 'there's no lock, and no key, and no bolt, and no door. There's no iron, nor no stone, no anything at all will keep me this night from the man I love.' And she went out into the moonlight to him, there by the bush where the flowers is pretty, beyond the river. And he says to her: 'You are all of the beauty of the world, will you come where I go, over the waves of the sea?' And she says to him: 'My treasure and my strength,' she says, 'I would follow you on the frozen hills, my feet bleeding.'

"Then they went down into the sea together, and the moon made a track upon the sea, and they walked down it; it was like a flame before them. There was no fear at all on her; only a great love like the love of the Old Ones, that was stronger than the touch of the fool. She had a little white throat, and little cheeks like flowers, and she went down into the sea with her man, who wasn't a man at all. She was drowned, of course. It's like he never thought that she wouldn't bear the sea like himself. She was drowned, drowned.

"When it come light they saw the seal-man sitting yonder on the rock, and she by him, dead, with her face as white as a flower. He was crying and beating her hands to bring life to her. It would have drawn pity from a priest to hear him, though he wasn't Christian. And at last, when he saw that she was drowned, he took her in his arms and slipped into the sea like a seal. And he swam, carrying her, with his head up, laughing and laughing and laughing, and no one ever saw him again at all."

Port of Many Ships

JOHN MASEFIELD

"Down in the sea, very far down, under five miles of water, somewhere in the Gulf of Mexico, there is a sea cave, all roofed with coral. There is a brightness in the cave, although it is so far below the sea. And in the light there the great sea-snake is coiled in immense blue coils, with a crown of gold upon his horned head. He sits there very patiently from year to year, making the water tremulous with the threshing of his gills. And about him at all times swim the goggle-eyed dumb creatures of the sea. He is the king of all the fishes, and he waits there until the judgement day, when the waters shall pass away for ever and the dim kingdom disappear. At times the coils of his body wreathe themselves, and then the waters above him rage. One folding of his coil will cover a sea with ship-wreck; and so it must be until the sea and the ships come to an end together in that serpent's death-throe.

"Now when that happens, when the snake is dying, there will come a lull and a hush, like when the boatswain pipes. And in that time of quiet you will hear a great beating of ships' bells, for in every ship sunken in the sea the life will go leaping to the white bones of the drowned. And every drowned sailor, with the weeds upon him, will spring alive again; and he will start singing and beating on the bells, as he did in life when starting out upon a cruise. And so great and sweet will be the music that they make that you will think little of harps from that time on, my son.

"Now the coils of the snake will stiffen out, like a rope stretched taut for hauling. His long knobbed horns will droop. The golden crown will roll from his old, tired head. And he will lie there as dead as herring, while the sea will fall calm, like it was before the land appeared, with never a breaker in her. Then the great white whale, old Moby Dick, the king of all the whales, will rise up from his quiet in the sea, and go bellowing to his mates. And all the whales in the world—the sperm-whales, the razor-back, the black-fish, the rorque, the right, the forty-barrel Jonah, the narwhal, the hump-back, the grampus and the thrasher—will come to him, 'fin-out', blowing their spray to the heavens. Then Moby Dick will call the roll of them, and from all the parts of the sea, from the north, from the south, from Callao to Rio, not one whale will be missing. Then Moby Dick will trumpet, like a man blowing a horn, and all that company of whales will 'sound' (that is, dive), for it is they that have the job of raising the wrecks from down below.

"Then when they come up the sun will just be setting in the sea, far away to the west, like a ball of red fire. And just as the curve of it goes below the sea, it will stop sinking and lie there like a door. And the stars and the earth and the wind will stop. And there will be nothing but the sea, and this red arch of the sun, and the whales with the wrecks, and a stream of light upon the water. Each whale will have raised a wreck from among the coral, and the sea will be thick with them—row-ships and sail-ships, and great big seventy-fours, and big White Star boats, and battleships, all of them green with the ooze, but all of them manned by singing sailors. And ahead of them will go Moby Dick, towing the ship Our Lord was in, with all the sweet apostles aboard of her. And Moby Dick will give a great bellow, like a fog-horn blowing, and stretch 'fin-out' for the sun away in the west. And all the whales will bellow out an answer. And all the drowned sailors will sing their chanties, and beat the bells into a music. And the whole fleet of them will start towing at full speed towards the sun, at the edge of the sky and water. I tell you they will make white water, those ships and fishes.

"When they have got to where the sun is, the red ball will swing open like a door, and Moby Dick, and all the whales, and all the ships will rush through it into an anchorage in Kingdom Come. It will be a great calm piece of water, with land close aboard, where all the ships of the world will lie at anchor, tier upon tier, with the hands gathered forward, singing. They'll have no watches to stand, no ropes to coil, no mates to knock their heads in. Nothing will be to do except singing and beating on the bell. And all the poor sailors who went in patched rags, my son, they'll be all fine in white and gold, And ashore, among the palm-trees, there'll be fine inns for the seamen, where you and I, maybe, will meet again, and I spin yarns, maybe, with no cause to stop until the bell goes."